AN EVENING TO REMEMBER
1777 SOCIETY

This book is a work of fiction. The names, characters, places, and incidents are products of the writer's imagination or have been used fictitiously and are not to be construed as real. Any resemblance to persons, living or dead, actual events, locales or organizations is entirely coincidental.

An Evening to Remember, 1777 Society, Book 3
Copyright © 2025 by Tamara Gill
Cover Art by Wicked Smart Designs
Editor Grace Bradley Editing, LLC

All rights reserved. Without limiting the rights under copyright reserved above, no part of this publication may be reproduced, stored in or introduced into a database and retrieval system or transmitted in any form or any means (electronic, mechanical, photocopying, recording or otherwise) without the prior written permission of both the owner of copyright and the above publishers.

ISBN: 978-1-923245-74-7

CHAPTER ONE

Kent, 1777

Matilda strolled around the mahogany dining table, her fingers brushing the polished edge as her gaze swept over the morning spread. A lavish assortment of delicacies greeted her: light pastries glazed with honey and dusted with sugared almonds, slices of tender ham cured with fragrant juniper, and soft eggs whipped into a rich custard before being baked in ceramic pots. Her mouth watered at the sight, and the tempting aroma emanating from the fruit centerpiece only heightened her anticipation.

Lady Charlotte, her dearest friend, had outdone herself with this wedding breakfast. The occasion to celebrate a second ceremony uniting Charlotte and Lord Lacy. A charming, intimate affair held in the family's ancestral chapel on their sprawling estate in Kent. Golden light filtering through leaded windows had cast a glow over the beautiful couple taking their vows, making the day feel as if it had been touched by heaven itself.

Matilda reached for a ripe strawberry, the bright-red fruit gleaming like a polished ruby atop a silver platter. Leaning casually against the walnut-paneled wall, she popped the berry into her mouth, closing her eyes as the sweetness burst on her tongue, mingling with the faint tang of lemon from the custard tart she'd savored earlier. For a moment, she allowed herself to revel in the simple pleasure, shutting out the growing unease that had taken root in her heart.

Her thoughts wandered to her friends—Genevieve, now blissfully married and preparing for the arrival of her first child, and Charlotte, glowing with the happiness of newlywed life. The realization that she alone remained unwed among their trio brought a sharp pang of melancholy. She sighed and picked up a morsel of quince jelly spread over a slice of bread, hoping the sweetness might dull the ache of her musings.

A sudden commotion from the gardens drew her attention. Laughter and the murmur of delighted voices floated through the open windows, mingling with the faint trill of a lark in the distance. Curious, Matilda moved through the dining room into the adjacent drawing room. The space was as grand as one might expect of a country estate. The walls were adorned with gilded portraits of past generations, their stern gazes softened by the flickering candlelight from ornate sconces. Heavy crimson drapes framed tall windows, and a marble fireplace dominated one end of the room, its mantel crowded with delicate porcelain figurines.

She stepped onto the stone terrace and shaded her eyes against the midday sun. Below, on the sweeping lawn bordered by rose bushes, a small crowd had gathered. At its center stood a figure unfamiliar to her—tall and broad-shouldered, his presence commanding even in the relaxed atmosphere of the family gathering. His dark riding coat was dusty from travel, his tan breeches clinging to muscular thighs, and his boots bore the scuffs of long hours in the saddle. There was an air of ruggedness about him, a stark contrast to the meticulously groomed gentlemen celebrating her friend's marriage who surrounded him.

Charlotte's delighted exclamation carried to her. "Christopher! You've come!"

Charlotte's brother, who returned from Scotland after years of absence seemed so different from the boy she vaguely remembered. Matilda watched as he kissed Charlotte's cheek, clasped Lord Lacy's shoulder in a brotherly embrace, and exchanged warm greetings with his parents. Her gaze lingered on him, noting the way his unkempt dark curls framed a strong, angular face. His eyes, the color of polished mahogany, gleamed with genuine affection as he laughed.

She swallowed a strange heat pooling in her chest. He looked nothing like the foppish beaux she'd encountered during the Season and certainly nothing like the boy she knew as a child. No, this man exuded vitality and purpose.

He turned suddenly, his gaze locking on her with startling intensity. Matilda froze, feeling as though he had stripped away her composure with that single, assessing glance. Heat crept up her neck, and she hastily looked away, fumbling for another strawberry to eat.

She forced herself to remain still when he strode toward her moments later. Charlotte was at his side, her expression alight with mischief and joy.

"Christopher, you remember my dearest friend, Lady Matilda Lane-Fox. Matilda, my brother, Lord Christopher Wright, Marquess Charteris."

His bow was exact, and when he took her hand, the warmth of his lips brushing her glove sent a shiver racing up her spine. "Lady Matilda," he said, his voice a deep rumble that made her breath catch. "It is a pleasure to meet you."

"The pleasure is mine, Lord Charteris," she managed, her words steady despite her racing heart. Up close, he was even more imposing—broad shoulders filling the space beside her, and his sharp features softened by the faint smile tugging at his lips.

"I understand you've only just returned from

Scotland," she ventured, hoping to prolong the exchange. "Do you reside there often?"

"Permanently," he replied, his tone clipped. "My father's northern estate demands it."

She opened her mouth to ask more, but his attention had drifted elsewhere. Disappointment pricked at her, and she stepped back, murmuring a polite excuse before retreating into the house.

Her heart sank as she watched him disappear into the throng of guests on the lawn. It seemed the enigmatic Lord Charteris had little interest in her despite her initial hopes when they locked eyes. Yet, despite his apparent indifference, her thoughts lingered on him—on the way his presence had filled the space around her and the brief flicker of warmth in his gaze before it had cooled.

For now, she would let him be. But something told her their paths would cross many times since they were both staying at this estate, and when they did, she intended to learn more about the man who had so unexpectedly captured her interest.

CHAPTER TWO

Christopher tossed and turned in his bed, the soft linen of his bedshirt clinging uncomfortably to his damp skin. Heavy with the day's accumulated heat, the room pressed in on him, the air stagnant and suffocating. In frustration, he threw off the bedding and climbed out of bed, the wooden floor cool under his bare feet as he crossed to the window. Lifting the sash, he sighed in relief as a soft, whispering breeze brushed over him, kissing his overheated skin.

The room itself offered no solace. Though luxurious, the heavy damask bed curtains trapped the heat, and even the faint glow of moonlight filtering through the gauzy inner drapes couldn't dispel the oppressive weight of the night. The faint creak of floorboards beneath his weight was the only sound, save for the distant chirp of crickets beyond the walls.

Leaning against the window frame, he gazed out at the estate bathed in silver moonlight. His eyes settled on the pond nestled within the gardens, its surface gleaming like molten glass under the celestial glow. The thought of cool water, beckoning and serene, was too tempting to ignore.

They needed a good storm to wash away the oppressive weather they'd been suffering through for days now. His mind wandered to Scotland, and when he would return there. At least in the Highlands, he didn't have to suffer such insufferable heat.

Decision made, he threw on his breeches, a shirt and boots, and slipped out of the room. The quiet corridors of the house, dark and empty, seemed almost conspiratorial as he made his way toward the terrace.

As he stepped outside, the night air was a balm to his heated skin. The gardens stretched before him, their shapes softened and dreamlike in the moonlight. Memories of childhood swam unbidden to his mind—of carefree days spent splashing in the pond with Charlotte, her laughter ringing out as their mother guided them on how to swim. Those days of innocence seemed a lifetime ago, overshadowed now by the burdens of adulthood and duty.

Reaching the pond, he strode onto the small pier, the wood damp under his boots. Kicking them off, he stripped away his breeches, leaving only his shirt, and dove into the water. The shock of the cool embrace sent a shiver through him, and his overheated body instantly soothed. Floating on his back, he let his arms drift outward, the gentle ripple of water lapping at his skin. Above him, the stars stretched endlessly, their twinkle a stark contrast to the restless thoughts still churning in his mind.

"Lord Charteris, is that you?"

The voice startled him, breaking the stillness. He flailed momentarily, righting himself in the water as his eyes searched for the source. Near the pier, a figure stood waist-high in the pond—a woman, her wet hair clinging to her shoulders, the moonlight casting her in a soft, ethereal glow.

"Lady Matilda?" he sputtered, his heart pounding as much from surprise as from the sight before him. "What on earth are you doing here at this hour? Do you not know how dangerous it is to swim alone?"

Her wide eyes narrowed before she rolled them, the defiant gesture igniting a spark of irritation within him. "I could ask the same of you, my lord." She crossed her arms, clearly irritated.

Her boldness caught him off guard, and he found himself at a loss for words. She moved quickly into the water, her shift plastered to her form, revealing curves that no gentleman ought to notice in polite company. Yet here, under the moonlight, she was no longer simply Lady Matilda, the dutiful Duke Lane-Fox's daughter—

she was a vision, a wet, gleaming goddess who appeared utterly unaffected by propriety or his growing unease.

And other appendages that seemed to be growing beneath the water's surface...

"I'm a man," he said finally, the feeble response leaving his lips before he could stop it.

"Well, I'm a woman," she replied, grinning with amusement, "and I can swim just as well as you." With that, she pushed off, rolling onto her back, her face upturned to the heavens. The water lapped at her, teasing the edges of her damp hair and caressing her bare shoulders.

Christopher swam closer, though he wasn't sure why. The sight of her, so uninhibited, sent a wave of something hot coursing through him. Her shift clung to her, the wet fabric translucent in places, and he struggled to keep his gaze on her face.

"What if you got into trouble and no one was here to save you?" His tone was strained, even to his own ears.

"Then I suppose I would have died," she answered matter-of-fact.

He stared at her, horrified. "That is a rather macabre thing to say, Lady Matilda."

She shrugged, and the movement caused the strap of her shift to slip down her arm, exposing the smooth curve of her collarbone. Without thinking, he reached out, his fingers brushing her skin as he pulled the fabric back into place. The contact was fleeting, yet it left him reeling.

Her eyes met his, wide and unguarded, and for a moment, the world seemed still. The soft sound of the water, the distant rustle of leaves, the very air around them—all of it faded, leaving only the connection they had shared.

"You must be pleased to be home," she said softly. "We didn't get to speak much today. Did you enjoy the wedding breakfast?"

Christopher welcomed the change of subject. "I'm very pleased to be home and visiting with my family. I reside mostly in Scotland, but could not miss my sister's wedding." He paused. "Although, the warmness here is...unfamiliar. I'm not certain I can withstand staying too long if one never gets relief from this heat, not even at night."

"Your family seemed very pleased you're home," she agreed. "As for the weather, I do not recall such stifling days in recent years, but it does make for lovely swims at night with friends."

He chuckled, supposing that was true. "So we're friends now, are we?"

She grinned but ignored his question. "You're ten years older than Charlotte, are you not?"

"I am." He treaded water as he watched her. She floated effortlessly, her expression serene. "And you're not married?" she asked, the question as bold as her presence was here this evening.

The unexpectedness of it made him laugh. "No, I'm not. Are you?"

"Would I be in a pond at this hour, with you, my lord, dressed like this if I were?" she retorted, a teasing smile curving her lips. Lips that made him forget himself or whatever the hell they were talking about.

He couldn't help but smile, though his amusement was tinged with disbelief. "I certainly hope you would not." Who was this woman? She was nothing like the perfect, polished debutante he had expected. And she was certainly different to the child he'd once known before he came of age. Instead, she was wild and untamed and, God help him, an utterly fascinating minx he did not want to cease speaking to. "Maybe you would," he countered, his cadence dry though his heartbeat quickened. "If you were up to no good."

"No good?" Her laugh, soft and melodic, danced over the water. "You mean if I were meeting a lover in the middle of the night, unbeknownst to my husband, who lies asleep indoors?" Her words were scandalous, her delivery maddeningly composed.

"You should not say such things when you do not know what they mean," he snapped, intending to chastise her. But her laughter deepened, a rich, velvety sound that seemed to wrap around him and settle low in his stomach.

Blast it all to hell. He needed to get a grip on himself.

"Oh, but I do know what happens between a man and a woman, my lord. I'm three and twenty, and I have read extensively," she challenged, her eyes sparkling with defiance and amusement. "There is little you could say or do that would shock me. I'm not as innocent as people believe."

"Truly?" His arms crossed over his chest, his posture feigned indifference, though he felt anything but. "Tell me more of your scandalous adventures. I'm all ears." His words were laced with sarcasm.

Her teasing smile faltered for the first time that evening, and already he missed it. She narrowed her eyes, her playful demeanor shifting into something sharper. "Well, now that my friends are married, I suppose I can admit to sneaking out of balls and parties and attending events in town that were not for the faint of heart. Have you heard of Lady Fraser's events? Her masques are very enlightening, indeed."

Christopher stiffened. Lady Fraser's events? He had heard of them, and they were anything but proper. They were risqué and for the demimonde, not haute *ton*. His throat tightened. What the devil had she been doing there?

"I have also been to Lady Dames's gambling hell a time or two," she added, her tone casual, though her eyes gleamed with challenge. "And as I said, I've read extensively. I know what you hint at, my lord, and while you may be trying to shock and ridicule me, shaming me for swimming and cooling off at night just as you are, all you're doing is making me more determined to do as I please." She met his eyes, and his heart, he was certain, ceased to beat.

How beautiful she was...

"I'm a curious person, and I like to stay informed. There is nothing wrong with that."

"More curious and informed about what?" he asked unable to swim away from her, even though for propriety sake he should.

Her laughter came again, soft and teasing. "I've seen how you look at me, my lord. You, like so many others, think I am some innocent lady who needs tutelage and guidance. I need none of those things. I am a woman with womanly wants and needs—just as you are a man with the same emotions. Do not heckle me, or you may be disparaged in return."

Her words struck him like a physical blow, their raw honesty stripping away the polished layers of propriety he clung to. He stared at her, his mouth dry, the cool water no longer enough to temper the heat coursing through him.

"This conversation is inappropriate." He cleared his throat. "I think you ought to return to the house, Lady Matilda before another word is spoken."

"Or you could leave." She stood in the water, raising an imperious brow, her smirk returning in full force. "I was here first, after all."

"You are also a guest, and this is my house," he retorted, his frustration bubbling to the surface. Why were they arguing like children? And why did he feel so utterly intrigued by her every word, every glance?

She tilted her head, the water cascading off her hair and shoulders like molten silver. "And are you going to make me?"

Dear Lord in heaven, was he?

CHAPTER
THREE

Matilda sat at the breakfast table the following morning, the faint clinking of porcelain mingling with the soft hum of conversation filling the room. The aroma of freshly brewed tea wafted through the air, along with the buttery scent of warm rolls. She cradled her delicate cup, the warmth seeping into her hands as she sipped and watched Charlotte and Lord Lacy exchange tender glances, their affection as evident as the golden light streaming through the window.

A wistful sigh escaped her lips. She longed for such a connection, for a kindhearted and forward-thinking gentleman. She could never wed a man who viewed his wife as a decorative piece, a mere vessel for heirs, to be seen but never heard. The thought of such a confined and unfulfilled existence set her teeth on edge.

No, she wanted more. She dreamed of Seasons filled with grand balls and lively soirées, where she could dance until her feet ached and converse with friends until dawn broke the horizon. She envisioned a family, children raised with compassion and a progressive spirit, nurtured in a household filled with warmth and laughter. But where could she find such a rare gentleman? Her closest friends seemed to have captured the last of London's suitable bachelors.

Perhaps Scotland held better prospects...

Her gaze wandered down the table to where Lord Charteris sat, his tall frame half-obscured by the morning paper. His perfectly sculpted features peeked over the edge, a chiseled jawline that could have been carved from marble. The memory of the previous evening at the lake flitted through her mind, and heat kissed her cheeks. She had seen far more of him than propriety allowed, and what she had glimpsed left little to be desired.

Not that he had been pleased to find her swimming in his lake. His dark scowl had spoken volumes. And his chastisement was a little stinging. Still, she had no intention of curbing her habits, especially with Charlotte so delightfully absorbed in her new husband, leaving her much free time to do as she pleased.

And she pleased to swim alone at night in the lake.

"I've asked Billy to saddle Major for you this morning, Matilda." Charlotte threw her a warm smile, brimming with affection. "Major will keep you safe, and you should have a pleasant ride around the estate."

Before Matilda could respond, the rustle of paper drew her attention. Lord Charteris folded the sheet with deliberate precision and slapped it onto the table, his movements brisk. He reached for his knife and fork, focusing more on his breakfast than the conversation at hand.

"Thank you, Charlotte," Matilda replied, eager to be away and free on horseback. "I'm looking forward to a long ride. It has been some time since I've been in the country, and one cannot enjoy horseback riding in town as much as one does here."

"Should you allow Lady Matilda on Major? He's seventeen hands, Charlotte," Lord Charteris interjected, his deep, resonant voice cutting through the quiet hum of the room. The rich timbre sent an unexpected shiver across Matilda's skin.

Was that concern she heard? She glanced at him, his sharp profile shadowed in the morning light. Perhaps beneath his gruff exterior lay a kernel of care—a begrudging consideration that he masked with curt remarks.

"Major will not throw Matilda," Charlotte assured them both, her smile unwavering. "He's steady, not flighty, and never eager to travel faster than a walk. Do not fret needlessly over my friend."

"Perhaps Dolly or Cool would be a better

choice," Lord Charteris suggested, his brow furrowing.

"Your mares?" Charlotte chuckled, her eyes sparkling. "They're far more likely to throw her—temperamental creatures, as you well know."

Matilda laughed, feeling a kinship with the spirited animals. "If you think Major will do well for me, I'm happy to take him."

"I will escort you," Lord Charteris announced, leaving no room for argument. "I need to check on the tenant farms near the western boundary. That will give you the long ride you're so eager for, Lady Matilda."

There was something about the way he said long ride—a subtle weight in his words that made the fine hairs at the nape of her neck stand on end. It wasn't unpleasant, but it left her momentarily breathless.

With the morning sun now casting a warm glow over the estate, conversations from the breakfast table dissolved into plans for the day.

By the time Matilda stepped into the stable yard, the warm morning air carried the faint scent of hay and leather, mingling with soft nickering of horses. Saddles were being tightened, hooves stomped against the ground, and soon, she and Lord Charteris were astride their mounts, the rolling countryside stretching wide before them.

Matilda didn't need to urge the gelding on very hard for the spirited animal to take the first hedgerow at a canter. Not as spirited as Charlotte made the gelding out to be... The rush of the affable morning air brushed her cheeks, carrying the faint, earthy scent of freshly tilled soil and wildflowers. The rhythmic thud of hooves against the soft earth was a comforting melody as they continued up the hill. Somewhere behind her, Lord Charteris trailed at a polite distance, allowing her the solitude she craved without the burden of small talk so many ladies found delightful.

She had little inclination to speak with his lordship. Unlike his sister, who was warm and welcoming, Lord Charteris exuded a guarded prickliness that set her on edge. His mere presence made her nervous, as though his dark, piercing eyes could uncover every thought she wished to keep hidden. She was never entirely certain if he liked her, even as a friend, though the question hardly mattered. He would soon be off to Scotland, leaving her free of his disconcerting scrutiny, and she would likely never see him again.

The distant thundering of hooves broke her thoughts as his lordship's horse came alongside hers, his deep baritone cutting through the tranquil morning. "You should not take hedgerows riding sidesaddle. It's not safe, Lady Matilda."

Matilda fought to suppress the frown threatening her features and instead reined her horse into a calm walk. The sun-dappled, rolling fields spread around them, and she forced herself to focus on the gentle rustle of leaves in the nearby copse rather than his admonishments. "My lord, while I thank you for your kind, concerned words, please know I've been riding for years. I am quite capable of jumping a hedgerow while riding sidesaddle. There's no need to fuss over me."

Her voice remained calm, though she injected enough determination into her words to match her resolve to do as she liked. She turned her gaze to admire the view—emerald hills dotted with grazing sheep and framed by a sky so blue it might have been painted.

"I do not want to be held responsible when you break your neck being reckless on a horse you've never ridden before," he persisted, his brows drawn in a frown. "It was bad enough you swim alone; nevertheless, now this."

Matilda drew in a deep breath, the scent of damp grass and distant woodsmoke grounding her. She tilted her head toward him, her expression deliberately placid. "I trust Charlotte's assurances about the temperament of her horse. Perhaps you ought to visit your tenant farmers now and leave me to my ride. I would hate to cause you undue stress."

"I'm not stressed." His reply was curt as he removed his top hat and raked a hand through his hair. Strands of dark brown, gleaming in the sunlight, fell back into place.

"Really? You seem quite upset."

She couldn't help the chuckle that escaped her lips, though she tried to disguise it as polite amusement. His dark eyes locked on to hers, the intensity of his gaze momentarily stealing her breath. Despite herself, she noted the sharp angles of his jawline and the way his features softened in the golden morning light. If only his personality were as agreeable as his appearance.

"You find this humorous? What if you had fallen and injured yourself? I doubt you would be laughing then, madam."

"Probably not," she admitted with a shrug, pulling her horse to a halt. "But I am neither a child to be chastised, nor a reckless fool. I am the daughter of a duke, a woman of three and twenty, not a girl in plaits learning to ride a pony. I do not need you to lecture me on the choices I make."

For a moment, he seemed on the verge of responding, but he hesitated, his lips parting before closing again. "Forgive me, Lady Matilda. I was merely concerned."

Her eyes softened as she studied him. His unease was almost endearing, though she still found his manner exasperating. "Do you always chastise your sister's friends? First the lake, and now my riding skills. What will it be next—my pianoforte playing or my card games?"

His dark brows furrowed, and he exhaled through his nose. "Your swimming in the lake was as reckless as this ride. You could have fainted, suffered a cramp, and drowned. Imagine if Charlotte had found you."

Matilda shook her head, not wishing that on

anyone, least of all her friend. "Then I would have been very sorry to cause her such pain. But one cannot live worrying about every possible mishap. We could sit here arguing about my recklessness, only for a tree limb to fall and crush us both. Do you see how absurd it is to live that way?"

"Perhaps," he conceded grudgingly, though his expression betrayed his lingering discomfort. "But I cannot help worrying when others fail to consider the risks of their actions."

"Truly, my lord, you should visit your tenants. I promise to finish my ride without further scandalous behavior." Her tone was light, though her words held a finality he couldn't ignore.

He studied her for a long moment, his dark eyes searching hers. "Why do I get the feeling you're trying to get rid of me?"

"Probably because I am." Her lips curved into a teasing smile. "You're far more perceptive than I gave you credit for."

Lord Charteris sighed, adjusting his seat in the saddle as he prepared to leave. "Do take care, Lady Matilda. These lands are unfamiliar to you, and the hedgerows are not as tame as they seem." He shook his head, clearly confounded by her. "I will meet you back here within the hour."

Matilda allowed her gaze to linger on his retreating form as he rode away, noting the easy grace with which he moved. A smile tugged at her lips. Perhaps he had a point about caution, but she would decide her own boundaries, as she always had.

She tightened her grip on the reins, her smile lingering as she turned her mount toward the open fields, the vast countryside promising the freedom she so fiercely cherished.

For the next hour, at least.

CHAPTER
FOUR

The rest of the day passed uneventfully, the house humming with the subdued activities of its occupants. Soon, the soft chime of the hallway clock signaled the hour to prepare for dinner. Matilda ascended the staircase, her slippers barely making a sound against the plush carpet before she changed into a gown of pale-blue silk, its fabric shimmering like a summer sky under the soft glow of candlelight. Her natural hair was set into an elegant upsweep adorned with delicate curls and ribbon accents, perfect for this evening's dinner party.

Once ready, she descended to the drawing room where the Duke and Duchess D'Estel were already present, speaking to Lord and Lady Haverly alongside their daughter, Lady Delphine, who, like herself, was unmarried and did not look to become so anytime soon.

They hailed from Surrey and were to dine with the family this evening. Lady Delphine was lovelier than Matilda remembered from several Seasons ago in London, not that she had remained long in town. The young woman had delicate features and a reserved demeanor that hinted at an innate elegance. Gathering her courage, Matilda approached the group, smoothing the folds of her gown as she offered a smile.

"Lady Matilda, may I present you to Lord and Lady Haverly and their daughter, Lady Delphine." The duchess smiled at each of them. "And will, in fact, be staying with us for the next week. I understand Lady Delphine is an avid horse rider, as you are, Matilda. I'm certain you'll enjoy many excellent outings together."

"I'm sure we shall," Matilda replied, dipping into a graceful curtsy. "It's lovely to meet you all."

Lady Delphine smiled but did not reply. Matilda hoped the young lady was merely shy and not unhappy that, she too, was a guest at the D'Estel estate.

The conversation turned to the hot weather, with the duchess lamenting the heat that had kept her indoors for much of the day, retreating to the terrace only as the sun sank low in the western sky. The murmurs of polite chatter filled the room, mingling with the soft clinking of glasses and the occasional flutter of fans as others joined pre-dinner drinks.

Charlotte slipped her arm through Matilda's, leading her to a quiet corner. "Lady Delphine is a spinster, seven and twenty, but she's exceedingly wealthy. They own half of Surrey, Papa says, yet she's never been presented at court and shows no interest in marrying. It's rather odd, do you not think?"

"Don't be so quick to judge, Charlotte. I may very well end up like Lady Delphine myself. I'll be four and twenty next year with no prospective husband in sight."

Charlotte frowned but shook her head determinedly. "I won't allow that to happen. Mark my words, you'll be married before the next Season is through. I'll see to it."

Matilda raised her brows at the statement. "Unless an eligible bachelor lurks in this house, I fail to see how that will come about."

Just then, Lord Charteris strode into the room. His confident gait faltered momentarily at the sight of Lady Delphine, a flicker of surprise and something akin to admiration crossing his features. Matilda's stomach tightened at the sight, an inexplicable pang of disappointment settling deep within her chest.

He bowed over Lady Delphine's hand, pressing a kiss to her gloved fingers in a polished and sincere gesture.

"Your brother seems quite taken with Lady Delphine," Matilda remarked in muted tones. "Perhaps he'll marry her, and I will be the only spinster left in England."

Charlotte snorted but followed Matilda's gaze toward her brother. "Highly unlikely, my dear. Christopher insists he won't marry unless he finds a love match—a deep, consuming passion that sweeps him off his feet. But if Father has his way, he'll have no choice who becomes his wife. He's ten years my senior, after all. He'll be an old man soon, and no one will want him."

Matilda studied Lord Charteris. He looked far from old. His tall, athletic frame and striking features were more akin to a Greek god than an aging, long-toothed bachelor. As he conversed with Lady Delphine, the woman's fluttering eyelashes and faint blush were telling.

"He doesn't seem so undesirable to Lady Delphine," Matilda noted. "She's blushing."

Charlotte glanced at the pair, her lips curving into a small smile. "We've known the Haverly family for years. Lady Haverly is a distant cousin of Mama's, which is why they visit so often. But I've never thought there was anything romantic between Lady Delphine and Christopher. Perhaps I was wrong. She does look rather smitten."

Matilda nodded, though an unfamiliar unease settled over her. Why should it matter to her if Lord Charteris found companionship with Lady Delphine? She had no interest in him herself—did she?

"Oh, did I mention?" Charlotte's voice interrupted her thoughts. "There's to be a ball at the local assembly rooms next Saturday. Mama's hosting, of course, so we'll have a night of dancing and revelry. It will be mostly townspeople and local gentry, but it should be a pleasant evening. Much less pompous than a London ball."

"Sounds perfect then," Matilda agreed, though her gaze drifted back to Lord Charteris and Lady Delphine. "They make a handsome pair, do you not think?"

"Perhaps," Charlotte conceded. "But I challenge there's anything between them."

"Really?" Matilda raised her brow, surprised by her friend's response. "Surely, there is a possibility for people's emotions to change over time. Maybe they like what they've seen here this evening, and it's the start of a grand love affair."

"No," Charlotte disagreed. "Christopher looks upon Lady Delphine as a sister and has done so for some years. The poor lady ought not to hope, for I would bet all my fortune that he sees her as a friend. He will only break her heart if she is living in hope of his beating for her."

Matilda looked back toward Lady Delphine, and again, the young woman appeared utterly smitten by Lord Charteris. A pang of pity filled Matilda, and she hoped that Charlotte was wrong for Lady Delphine's sake.

Dinner was announced, and hours later, Matilda finally escaped to her room. The lingering heat of the day had given way to a balmy evening, and the allure of the lake proved too irresistible. Matilda waited for the house to quieten and the last of the family and guests to retire, before she escaped outside. Sneaking out of her room, she made her way through the house toward the terrace doors before kicking off her slippers and dashing across the moonlit lawns, the damp grass cool beneath her feet.

She reached the dock and sat on the end, slipping her feet into the water, sighing as its cool embrace soothed her overheated skin. The quiet lap of waves against the wooden beams and the soft chirping of crickets created a symphony of tranquility.

How she loved this time of the night...

"Out here again, Lady Matilda? Didn't you retire two hours ago?"

She gasped, turning to see Lord Charteris approaching. His attire—or lack thereof—rendered her momentarily mute. Gone were the stiff cravat and polished boots; in their place, he wore only buckskin breeches and a loose shirt that revealed the strong lines of his shoulders.

"I could say the same for you," she replied, forcing her gaze back to the water.

He sighed and sat beside her, the dock creaking under his weight. Sliding his feet into the water, he stirred the surface idly. "At least I cannot fault you for this. No harm can come from merely cooling your feet."

She smiled, grateful for his lack of reprimands. "Lady Delphine seemed pleased to see you again. I understand you've known each other since childhood."

"Yes, for many years," he replied, his response carefully neutral. "She's older than Charlotte, but five years my junior."

"She never married. I wonder why?" Matilda ventured, curiosity getting the better of her.

Lord Charteris's jaw tightened. "You'd have to ask Lady Delphine. I'm not one to speculate on another's choices."

"Perhaps I will, since you won't tell me."

He turned to her, his dark eyes narrowing. "Must you know everything about everyone? You're quite the meddler."

"And must you be so secretive?" she countered.

Their gazes locked, and Matilda's breath hitched as his eyes dipped to her lips. The idea of kissing him swirled in her mind all of a sudden, and her stomach rolled with nerves. What would it feel like to kiss him? Would she enjoy it? Would he even allow such liberties?

"I find my secretive nature adds to my allure." His tone low and teasing. "You can't deny you're intrigued."

"I am," she admitted, "though perhaps not in the way you think."

"Really?" His brow arched. "Now I'm intrigued. Dare to tell?"

"Maybe." But even as she spoke, her thoughts betrayed her. She didn't want to tell him. She wanted to show him exactly how he bewitched her.

CHAPTER
FIVE

Christopher wasn't certain what had come over him. Perhaps it was the spell of the moonlit night, the gentle lapping of water against the dock, or the way Lady Matilda's presence seemed to consume the very air around him. Her delicate features, illuminated by the silvery light, were captivating. She looked at him now with an unspoken longing, her lips parted, her eyes shimmering with expectation. He could scarcely bear the thought of disappointing her.

From the moment he had met Lady Matilda, Christopher had been drawn to her in a way that both thrilled and unnerved him. She awakened a yearning he knew was perilous—a flame that, if left unchecked, might consume them both. He told himself he could not act on such desires, not until he was certain of his feelings, or had resolved the misunderstanding that plagued his every waking hour, a shadow from his past that loomed large over his present even now.

He could not drag Matilda into his life, make her believe that he could offer any form of future when he did not know himself what that future entailed. She was innocent of his past troubles, and he would be loath to drag her into his muddy here and now.

Yet, as Matilda leaned forward, her lashes fluttering shut, the space between them seemed to disappear. The way her soft breaths mingled with the crisp night air was intoxicating, her beauty almost unbearable. His restraint wavered, but his sense of duty—fragile as it was—still held. He couldn't. He wouldn't. Not until the chains of his past were broken.

But then her hands, warm and trembling, cupped his face, and the world fell away. At that moment, all rational thought vanished.

Christopher closed the space between them without hesitation, brushing his lips against hers in a tentative kiss. Relief surged through him, followed by a profound sense of rightness. He slid a hand to the nape of her neck, tipping her chin upward to deepen the kiss. Her lips, soft and inviting, met his eagerly, her inexperience evident but endearing. When his tongue skimmed hers, he felt her surprise—her hesitation—but soon, with her characteristic quickness, she mimicked his movements, matching him in an unspoken rhythm.

Desire roared through him like a tempest. His

carefully constructed walls crumbled, and he allowed himself to act on raw instinct for the first time in years. Their kiss was no mere meeting of lips; it was a collision of longing and passion, a searing exchange that left him both elated and undone. He pulled her closer, her slender frame fitting faultlessly against his. The thin fabric of her nightdress offered little barrier, her softness pressing against the hard planes of his chest, teased and tormented him.

His body reacted instinctively, his arousal impossible to ignore, but even as the fire within him burned hotter, he clung to his last shred of control. To go further would be unthinkable—a betrayal of everything he held sacred. He allowed himself the pleasure of her fingers tangling in his hair, the slight sting sending a heady mix of pain and pleasure through his veins. Still, it was enough to remind him of the line he could not— must not—cross.

With an effort that felt Herculean, Christopher broke the kiss, his breath ragged, his heart pounding against his ribs. The sight of Matilda's flushed face, her lips swollen from their embrace, nearly undid him again. But he pulled back, creating a necessary distance between them, though every fiber of his being screamed to close it.

"We must stop," he rasped. "This... This isn't right." Even as the words left his lips, he leaned forward, stealing one last, lingering kiss. "No, truly, Matilda, we cannot do this."

She tilted her head, a teasing smile curving

her lips. "It's only a kiss, my lord. I'm not expecting you to offer marriage."

Her casual response stunned him, and he wrenched farther away, needing the cool night air to clear his thoughts. "Have you ever been kissed before, my lady? Are you telling me you've done this with other men?"

The thought of another man tasting her lips, touching her as he had, sent an unwelcome surge of jealousy coursing through him.

"No, of course not," she replied with a hint of amusement. "You're the first. And I must say, I enjoyed it quite a lot. Perhaps you could bestow more kisses upon me—it would certainly make my stay here more...diverting."

Christopher stared, dumbfounded. "Are you saying kissing me is merely a pastime for you? I'm not sport, my lady." He stood, placing his hands on his hips.

She laughed in muted tones. Rising from the dock, she stepped close, her eyes glinting mischievously. "Of course not, my lord. But I'm also not asking for your hand in marriage. A kiss is simply a kiss. I'm perfectly content with leaving it at that."

Her honesty disarmed him, but it did little to calm the unease gnawing at his conscience. He should be relieved, yet the thought of her exploring such intimacy with another man filled him with a possessiveness he couldn't quite name.

"If you must kiss anyone, Lady Matilda, let it

be me," he said. "For your reputation's sake, of course."

"For my reputation," she echoed, grinning as she linked her arm through his. "But you are a very good kisser, my lord. Perhaps I could learn more from you—purely for educational purposes."

He chuckled despite himself, allowing her to guide him back toward the house. "For your future husband, I presume?"

"Precisely," she said, playfully, yet the idea of her kissing anyone made him uneasy. They stopped beneath the shadow of an ancient elm, and she tipped onto her toes and brushed her lips against his. The fleeting kiss left him breathless all over again.

"Goodnight, Lord Charteris," she whispered in a sultry note that lingered in the air long after she had disappeared into the house.

Christopher stood rooted to the spot, watching her retreat across the moonlit lawn. Even as he returned to his chamber, he was certain his wits were still scattered. Matilda had undone him, and he resolved to harden himself against her charms—for both their sakes.

Yet deep down, he already knew it was a battle he had little chance of winning.

CHAPTER SIX

Matilda spent the following day embroidering cushions alongside Charlotte, who was feeling unwell. Though her needle moved methodically through the fabric, her mind was elsewhere—filled with thoughts of Lord Charteris and their shared kiss. The memory played repeatedly in her mind, stirring emotions she couldn't entirely name.

She knew better than to believe it would happen again. Despite her playful hint that a kiss was not overly scandalous, she understood the truth of it all too well. The forbidden nature of their shared moment lingered heavily in her conscience. A kiss with anyone, let alone her best friend's brother, was a breach of the unspoken rules that governed her world.

But he was so very handsome. And with several weeks before she left for Genevieve's new home, she could hardly ignore how much more exciting he made the days. After all, there were only so many hours one could fill with horse riding, swimming, and embroidery.

Lady D'Estel sat near the window, her embroidery frame catching the soft afternoon light. Positioned a little apart, she gave Charlotte and Matilda enough distance to speak freely.

"Charlotte, dear," Matilda ventured in whispered tones, "may I ask a question about your brother?"

Charlotte stabbed her needle into the cushion and leaned back, resting her hands in her lap as she turned her full attention to her. "Of course. What would you like to know?"

Matilda hesitated, unsure how to frame her curiosity without revealing too much. "I suppose I'd like to know why he isn't married. He's a titled lord, bound to inherit a dukedom, and undeniably handsome. Why does he stay away from London and the throngs of ladies who, I'm sure, would eagerly pursue him during the Season?"

Charlotte shrugged, pursing her lips in thought. "I can't say for certain," she said in hushed tones, glancing at her mama. "But I believe it has something to do with our cousin, Frank Langley. If anything were to happen to Christopher, our cousin is next in line. He's married and has a son, so the line is secure. I, therefore, think Christopher likely feels no obligation to marry anytime soon. I think he rather enjoys the freedom of being an eligible bachelor."

"But in Scotland? Surely there is little society in the Highlands?"

Charlotte shrugged. "He spends a good deal of time in Edinburgh during the Season. Their society isn't as grand as London's, but it's still lively enough. Plenty of eligible matches to be found there."

Matilda paused her sewing, surprised. "Do you think he might be attached to someone in Scotland? Someone unsuitable, perhaps?"

Charlotte frowned at the cushion as she considered the notion. "I'd hate to think so—it would be terribly disappointing for him if that were the case, for our parents would not approve of the match." She paused. "But no, he's never shown any particular interest in anyone. I believe he's simply comfortable with his life as it is."

"And your parents? Doubtless, they wish for him to marry."

"You are correct, they do," Charlotte replied, glancing toward her mother. "Mama is desperate for him to marry and produce an heir. I think that's why she invited Lord and Lady Haverly and their daughter, Lady Delphine, to stay. Mama and Papa would be thrilled with such a match, but as I said before, I do not believe Christopher would be."

"Then I feel very sorry for your parents." Though her heart felt lighter with the knowledge. She returned to her embroidery, stitching a delicate pink tulip as her mind turned over Charlotte's words.

Was Lady Delphine here because both families hoped for a union between her and Lord

Charteris? If so, Matilda's kiss with him certainly did not bode well for the heiress.

The realization sent a pang of guilt through her. How terrible to have kissed a man who might be destined for another. Lady Delphine, thought quiet, was kind and a gentle soul, she believed. How could Matilda have been so thoughtless? Did this make her no better than a lightskirt? She resolved to do better, to resist the temptation of Lord Charteris's kisses—no matter how delectable they were.

She felt Charlotte's gaze and refused to meet her friend's eyes.

"Matilda, dear..." Charlotte's tone was laced with curiosity, "do your questions about my brother mean you have feelings for him? I love Lady Delphine, but I would prefer to call you my sister than anyone else."

Matilda's head snapped up, her cheeks flaming. "No, not at all," she insisted. "I was merely curious. He's of marriageable age—if not a bit past it, to be honest—and I wondered why such an eligible, handsome man hadn't wed."

"Handsome?" Charlotte teased, her lips curling into a smirk.

Before Matilda could respond, Lord Charteris strolled into the room, his presence commanding, even in its casualness. He popped a morsel of something into his mouth before slumping onto the settee between them. The heat that rushed to Matilda's face was instant and undeniable.

"As for why I'm unmarried," he said with a

roguish grin, "that is entirely my choice—just as it is your choice to remain unwed at three and twenty."

"You shouldn't eavesdrop on conversations, Christopher," Charlotte scolded.

"Hard not to," he replied with a shrug, "when you're not being the least bit discreet."

Matilda's heart pounded as she prayed no one else had overheard. The last thing she wanted was to seem overly curious—or worse, infatuated.

"I was about to ask if Lady Matilda would care for a ride before dinner," Lord Charteris continued. "The weather is agreeable, and we have a few hours yet before we dine. That is, of course, if she's finished discussing my life."

Charlotte sighed dramatically. "Take her, then. But take my maid with you as a chaperone."

Lord Charteris rolled his eyes as he stood. "I'm not going to compromise your friend, Charlotte. She's three and twenty, hardly in need of a chaperone."

"With you, I think she does," Charlotte countered with a grin.

Matilda laughed as she rose, but her stomach churned at the thought of their kiss last night. "I'll change and meet you at the stables, my lord." She left quickly, her heart fluttering as anticipation filled her chest.

As she made her way upstairs, Matilda

couldn't suppress the thrill of riding with him again.

We are friends and nothing more. The thought brought little comfort. Perhaps, during their ride, she might find the courage to ask him about Lady Delphine and his parents' plan for them both. Or perhaps...she wouldn't.

CHAPTER
SEVEN

Matilda followed Lord Charteris out of the stables, her horse trotting alongside his as they made their way around the lake. The sunlight glinted off calm water, and the gentle rustling of leaves in the breeze carried a faint, earthy scent of summer. The grand estate loomed in the distance, a stately backdrop to their casual ride along the water's edge.

"So, you think I'm handsome?" His lordship glanced at her, that wicked, teasing smile tugging at his lips.

Matilda shook her head, struggling to keep her composure as laughter bubbled just beneath the surface. Of all the things for him to recall! "There are many gentlemen I think handsome, my lord. You are merely one of them."

He chuckled, the sound low and rich, and turned his gaze ahead. The breeze lifted his hair, softening his otherwise godlike features. She bit back a smile, knowing all too well how frightfully attractive he was—and how aware of it he seemed to be.

"Well," he began, "you'll be pleased to know I've invited some friends from London to the assembly rooms ball this Saturday. Perhaps one of those London beaus will capture the elusive Lady Matilda's heart."

She snorted, shaking her head. "Unlikely, my lord. None of them managed to tempt me during the last Season in London. I doubt one evening at a country dance will make much difference."

"My friends might." His gaze dipped to her lips for a fleeting moment, and her stomach fluttered in response. "Several of my friends prefer the quieter delights of Whites or Brooks over the chaos of balls and parties. Some did not even attend the Season, choosing instead the peace of the country estates. They may surprise you."

She supposed they could. The thought of meeting unfamiliar gentlemen held a certain appeal, especially those not already dismissed from her consideration during the Season.

"I will admit," she said with a sigh, "that I'm rather picky these days. After seeing my friends marry for true, enduring love, I find my expectations have risen. I won't surrender my independence for anything less."

"A true, honorable gentleman should not ask a woman to lose her independence simply because he wished to marry her," he replied, his voice firm.

"Careful, Lord Charteris," she teased, "or you'll become dangerously enticing when you speak like that."

His laugh rumbled deep in his chest, a sound that sent a delightful prickle through her. She scolded herself.

Do not fall for his charms, Matilda. He's only a friend and nothing more.

"I'm sorry to disappoint you, my lady," he replied, his tone abruptly serious, "but I cannot offer my husbandly services, much as I enjoy your company." His gaze swept over the lands surrounding them, his expression shifting to one of quiet contemplation.

He looked every inch the nobleman, regal and composed. Matilda studied him, wondering what weighed so heavily on his mind. Why was he so resolute in his decision not to marry?

"I won't press you further." As much as she wished she could, she knew it was not right. "But I may sneak another kiss or two, if you allow. I did enjoy your tutelage the other day." His head snapped toward her, surprise flickering in his eyes. She shrugged, feigning nonchalance. "I'm forward, my lord, but it's the truth. Did you not enjoy kissing me?"

He shifted in his saddle, clearing his throat. "Of course I did. What man wouldn't? But we should not do so again. Recklessness rarely ends well, and I fear I lose my senses when I'm near you."

His admission pleased her more than it should have, but she schooled her expression into one of innocence. Nudging her horse closer, she leaned toward him. "We're alone now. There's no one to see us. Would you like to kiss me again here?"

"No. Definitely I do not." He looked away, though he made no effort to increase the distance between them.

"Come now, Christopher," she said, using his given name. "We've agreed you wish to remain a bachelor, and I wish to marry for love. Since our goals do not align, there's no harm in sharing another kiss. I am dreadfully bored, after all. Your sister is always occupied, and I find myself quite alone these days. Be my diversion until I leave, won't you?" She was being a terrible minx, but she could not help herself. There was something about Lord Charteris that made her throw caution to the wind.

"No," he said firmly, though his tone lacked conviction.

She frowned and reached out, clasping his reins and halting his horse. "I say yes."

He attempted to move forward again, but she stopped him. "Are you always this demanding? I'm not some libertine, Matilda."

She laughed, enjoying their banter. "Of course, you are not. It's just a kiss—not a scandal." She paused, studying him as a niggling suspicion would not dissipate. "Is it Lady Delphine who keeps you from kissing me?" she asked finally. "Your sister hinted your families have hopes of a match between you."

"No," he stated, his answer sharp, before he urged his mount forward. "We're friends, just as you and I are. I wouldn't raise her hopes for a match any more than I would you."

"But you're not raising my hopes," she countered, catching up and halting his horse again. "We're friends who sometimes kiss. There's no harm in that."

"I cannot kiss you again."

"Christopher." Her words were soft yet insistent. "I promise not to fall in love with you. Will that soothe your worries? I only want to kiss you again because...because you do it so well."

He stared at her, his expression unreadable. She felt her heart race, her stomach clench with expectation. "Kiss me, Christopher," she urged, barely above a whisper.

"Get off the horse," he ordered.

She dismounted quickly, her heart pounding as he did the same. Their horses flanked them, the towering animals shielding them from view. Christopher stepped closer, his hand slipping to the nape of her neck. "God damn you, Matilda. You make denying you impossible," he growled, as his lips brushed hers lightly at first, then pressed harder, capturing her in a kiss that stole her breath.

All rational thought fled as his arm circled her waist, pulling her flush against him. The firm planes of his chest pressed against her, and her fingers tangled in his hair, drawing him closer. His tongue teased, sending shivers wracking her every sense.

This—was what she craved. To feel alive, desired, and cherished, even for a fleeting moment. His kiss deepened, and she knew she would never forget how he made her feel.

And she never wanted to.

CHAPTER
EIGHT

Christopher needed to stop kissing Matilda, yet he could not tear his lips from her sweet mouth.

She kissed him with a passion that stole his breath and scattered his wits, leaving him bereft of reason. He doubted anything at this moment could separate him from her. She was intoxicating—so sweet, so perfectly molded to him that his entire body seemed to hum in her presence.

Her softness was a revelation, her pliant form pressing against him as though they were pieces of the same puzzle. She fit him like a glove, her curves aligning with his strength, her warmth seeping through their layers of clothing. She smelled of jasmine, delicate and tantalizing, a scent that seemed to wrap around him and tighten his resolve in the worst way.

Her hair, untamed by fashionable convention,

was tied back with a simple ribbon. Loose curls escaped their bindings, framing her flushed cheeks, her face alight with the glow of desire. In this golden hour of the late afternoon, she was radiant —a vision of beauty he wanted desperately to keep.

And yet, he knew he must stop.

He pulled her closer, his body betraying his mind's frantic cries for restraint. Every press of her lips against his sent his thoughts tumbling deeper into a haze of longing. He should halt this madness, but how could he when every part of him screamed to keep her close?

But the truth loomed, cold and unrelenting. He could not pursue her. He could not pursue anyone.

The weight of his past, of a foolish mistake that had followed him like a shadow, made that impossible. Here, at his family's estate, Lady Delphine was a constant reminder of that mistake. Her presence was like a persistent chill in the air after a summer storm, clinging to him no matter how hard he tried to shake it off.

Not that he believed himself in love with Matilda. But at three and thirty, he certainly had a better understanding of what he wanted in a wife—a companion who could stand beside him, a mother to his future children.

Love...

A low, throaty moan escaped her lips as his tongue brushed hers, a sound that ignited a fire within him. His body responded immediately, his arousal undeniable, urgent, and damnably inconvenient.

Damn it all to hell. He needed to put an end to this madness.

With a sharp breath, he broke the kiss and stepped back. Regret clawed at him as soon as the distance grew between them. "You should not kiss me—or anyone—unless you mean to marry them."

Her wide eyes stared up at him, sparkling with mischief and confusion. He should not chastise her, especially when he was as much a participant in these forbidden encounters as she. But desperation drove his words.

"You're an excellent teacher, my lord." Her eyes sparkled with defiance and amusement. "Think of it this way: when I do find the man I wish to marry, he'll be well-pleased with my kisses."

Her boldness left him momentarily stunned, though he shouldn't have been surprised. Matilda seemed to be a force of nature. Without waiting for his reply, she turned to her horse, leading it to a fallen tree. With an effortless grace that spoke of her independence, she used the trunk to climb into the saddle without assistance.

He mounted his horse as well, still grappling with the tumult of emotions her presence stirred in him. Her spirit, untamed and unyielding, was something he admired deeply. He prayed, not for the first time, that she would find a husband worthy of her—a man who would cherish her fire, not extinguish it.

The sound of approaching hooves broke his thoughts. Christopher glanced over his shoulder to see Lady Delphine cantering toward them, her posture flawless atop her bay mare.

Lady Delphine was undeniably beautiful. Her hair was the perfect chestnut shade that gleamed in the sunlight, her face framed by the soft curve of a fashionable bonnet. She had an elegance Society adored. But despite all her attributes, she stirred nothing in him. Not since their adolescent folly—when, during a ball, they had shared stolen champagne and a drunken kiss beneath a supper room table.

That childhood and childish foolish act had led to an even more foolish proposal—one born of youthful gallantry rather than genuine affection. She had accepted on the condition that they wait until they come of age and enter Society. Yet, despite the passage of years, she remained unmarried, as if the fanciful proposition was binding.

"Lord Charteris, Lady Matilda," she called to gain their attention. "Out for a ride, I see. I do wish you'd extended the invitation. I should have loved to join you."

"You're most welcome to join us now, Lady Delphine." Christopher forced a polite smile. "I hadn't realized you were about. I did not see you at breakfast."

Her lips curved into a smile that hinted at

hope. "I had a headache this morning," she explained before turning her attention to Matilda. "I bring a summons from the house, Lady Matilda. Lady Lacy requires your assistance with preparations for the assembly room ball this Saturday."

Matilda's shoulders sagged ever so slightly, though she maintained her composure. "Oh, she does? That is strange. I spoke to her not an hour before riding out, and she mentioned nothing of it. But perhaps something urgent has arisen." With a soft sigh, she turned her horse toward the house.

Christopher seized the opportunity. "Would you like me to escort you, Lady Matilda?"

"The house is within sight, my lord. Lady Matilda will be perfectly safe," Lady Delphine interjected smoothly. "Besides, I would dearly enjoy a full turn about the lake—if you'd escort me."

Matilda hesitated, glancing between them before nodding. "As Lady Delphine says, I shall be well. Good afternoon to you both." With that, Matilda nudged her horse into a canter, disappearing down the path back toward the estate.

Lady Delphine turned to him, her smile unnervingly calculated. "Now that we're alone at last, Lord Charteris, I must say how much I've missed our time together. Why must you stay away for years in cold, dreary Scotland?" She pouted for effect, which did not work.

Christopher forced his voice to remain even.

"Our Scottish estate is as important as our English one. With my father managing affairs here, it falls to me to oversee the tenants and servants there. It would be remiss of me as a gentleman to neglect them for the frivolities of town."

"But if you spent more time in England, we might see each other more often," she countered. "Is that not what you want?"

"Lady Delphine, we were children when we shared such closeness you speak of. We have both grown since then. Surely it is time to look to the future rather than dwell on the past."

Her face flushed, but she held her ground. "Are you saying you no longer intend to honor the promise you made me all those years ago?"

Christopher sighed, the noose around his neck tightened. He would need to tread carefully before she flew into a fit of the vapors.

"We were children, Lady Delphine. Surely you do not still cling to the feelings of your youth. Doubtless, there is another who has caught your heart," Christopher said, anxiety coiling in his chest.

Her pretty features flushed a mottled pink, and her lip trembled as her composure wavered. She pulled out a delicate lace-trimmed handkerchief embroidered with her initials and dabbed at her eyes and nose.

"I feel the same as I always have." She paused, gathering her composure. "I thought you were not the sort of man who would lead a woman astray with false feelings. Do you not want to marry me anymore, Lord Charteris? I have waited so long for you to broach the subject again, and I cannot wait any longer. I am seven and twenty—I'm almost too old to have children. Are you going to do the right thing by me since it was you who asked for my hand in the first place?"

Christopher stared at her, his thoughts a whirlwind. He had never anticipated this moment, though perhaps he should have. He struggled to reconcile her earnest expression with the stark reality that such a union would be disastrous for them both.

He did not love her. The truth settled like a stone in his gut, heavy and immutable. And to marry her out of obligation would only result in pain—for her, as much as for himself.

"Are you saying that you are holding me to my proposal—one I made at but sixteen years of age?" he asked, baffled by her resolve.

"I am, yes." She lifted her chin with an air of defiance. The trembling of her lip had ceased, replaced by a steely determination that made her look almost regal. "What say you, my lord?"

Christopher inhaled deeply, the warm summer air doing little to clear his mind. He needed to choose his words carefully, though no answer would save him from the web he had spun.

"I suppose, as a gentleman, you are leaving me with little choice but to agree, are you not?"

His words sounding resigned, even to his own ears.

"That is true, my lord," she said, her lips curving into a small, victorious smile. "I am pleased to hear we have finally come to an agreement. Now, there is only one thing left for us to do."

Christopher inwardly cringed, tightening his grip on the reins. His horse shifted beneath him as though sensing his unease. "And what is that?"

"Tell our families, of course, of the happy news. We should start back directly. There is so much to plan and do, and we shall have such a merry time planning our wedding." She nudged her mount into a walk, her movements brisk with purpose. "And just think," she added, glancing over her shoulder at him gleefully, "I shall be able to return with you to Scotland. I've never been and shall love it as much as I love you."

Christopher's stomach churned as he followed her, his horse's hooves crunching against the gravel path with a rhythmic finality. Each step toward the house felt like another turn of the noose tightening around his neck.

"Sounds like you have everything planned, but I think we must delay the announcement. Just for a short time. The news of our youthful folly will shock my parents, and I will require time to think of how to breach the subject with them." He watched her, hoping she would agree, so instead of doing the latter, he could figure out a way to get himself out of this mess.

She threw him a mischievous grin, her spirits buoyed by his capitulation. "Of course, my lord. All will be just as I hoped once your parents get over the initial shock." She paused. "I have no qualms in waiting. I've waited ten years already, what is another few weeks?"

He nodded, yet he could not force a smile. Not this time. "As you say."

CHAPTER NINE

Matilda returned to the house, her mood unnervingly sour after leaving Lord Charteris and Lady Delphine alone, only to find that Charlotte had not asked for her at all and was currently not to be disturbed in her suite of rooms.

"Are you certain Charlotte's not asked for me?" Matilda questioned her friend's maid, amending her tone when it came out more clipped than was necessary. "I've just returned from my ride because Lady Delphine said Charlotte requested my assistance."

The maid frowned, a faint crease marring her otherwise smooth brow. "No, my lady. I'm sorry, but Lady Lacy has not left her room this morning, and I know for certain Lady Delphine has not seen her ladyship since last evening. I think there must be some kind of oversight."

"Of course. Thank you," Matilda replied with forced politeness, though her blood simmered beneath her calm exterior. Turning toward her room, she reminded herself that she needed to change out of her riding habit before anything else could be done about the lie Lady Delphine had spoken to her just a short time before.

Once inside, her maid helped her into a comfortable day dress of pale lavender muslin with delicate white trim at the cuffs and hem. The light fabric was soft against her skin, but it did little to soothe her irritation. Crossing to the window, she pulled back the sheer curtain and looked out onto the sprawling grounds of the D'Estel estate.

From her vantage point, she spotted Lord Charteris and Lady Delphine still some distance from the house. Their horses walked docilely beside each other, their heads low and steps unhurried, while the riders engaged in what appeared to be a congenial conversation.

A pang of jealousy and annoyance shot through her, sharp and unwelcome. To be called away from her ride for a summons that proved false was not the act of a lady. Such trickery spoke of a lack of decorum and breeding, a violation of the very etiquette they had all been raised to uphold.

Matilda narrowed her eyes, her gaze fixed on Lady Delphine. The woman was undeniably beautiful, her red hair a glossy cascade beneath her riding hat, her figure graceful atop her mount. She was as eligible as Matilda for any lord or gentleman with sufficient wealth to satisfy their ambitious fathers. Yet Matilda couldn't shake the feeling that this was more than a simple misunderstanding.

Lady Delphine's intent seemed clear. She had her cap set on Lord Charteris and saw Matilda as an obstacle to be removed. The thought burned in Matilda's chest, though she told herself it was the deception—not the man in question—that stung.

Turning abruptly from the window, Matilda left her room, her steps brisk as she headed downstairs to the billiards room. It was a place she could be sure no one else would frequent at this hour. The thought of striking a few balls around the table seemed an ideal way to channel her frustration without confronting Lady Delphine outright.

The faint scent of beeswax polish mingled inside the room with the earthy aroma of aged wood. Dust motes swirled in the sunlight streaming through the tall windows, their golden glow softening the dark green baize of the billiard table. Matilda selected a cue and began lining up multiple shots, telling herself her disrupted ride and love of the outdoors had soured her mood.

But she knew that wasn't the truth.

She had been enjoying Lord Charteris's company more than she had expected. Their shaky start had given way to an unexpected camaraderie, and after two astonishing kisses, she found herself longing for more—not just of his kisses but of his presence and conversation.

She did not want him as a husband. No, of course, she did not.

Yet the idea of him marrying Lady Delphine grated on her. Not after such blatant trickery.

The door creaked open behind her, and she struck the ball harder than necessary, sending it clattering into the pocket. She turned to see the very man who occupied too much of her thoughts entering the room, his broad shoulders framed by the light spilling in from the hallway. He shut the door behind him and froze when he realized he was not alone.

Surprise flickered across his handsome features. He stood there for several heartbeats, his gaze dipping to her lips.

Without warning, a reckless impulse seized her, and she set down her cue stick and strode toward him. Without giving herself time to reconsider, she clasped his jaw, rose onto her tiptoes, and kissed him.

His response was immediate and all that she could hope for. He pulled her into his arms, his grip firm yet achingly gentle. The passion in his kiss stole her breath, scattering her senses like leaves in a tempest.

"Matilda..." Her name a plea against her lips, as he guided her back toward the billiard table.

Her bottom hit the edge, and before she could draw another breath, Christopher lifted her onto the table, settling himself between her legs.

She had never been in such a position before. No man had ever stood so boldly between her thighs, nor had she allowed anyone such liberties.

But she couldn't summon the will to push him away. She didn't want to.

At three and twenty, she knew this moment might be her only opportunity to experience such passion. If no man ever captured her heart and offered her marriage, then at least she would have this.

This one memory in his arms.

Her hands clutched his riding coat, pulling him closer. His scent—earthy leather mingled with the faint scent of their afternoon ride—enveloped her, heightening her senses.

"Christopher," she moaned as his warm, calloused hand slipped under her dress along her calf, lifting her knee against his hip. The roughness of his palm against her skin sent heat pooling deep within her core.

"You're driving me to distraction." He vibrated with barely held restraint as he pressed against her. The friction stole her breath, obliterating all sense of propriety.

His other hand moved to her bodice, his fingers grazing the soft swell of her breast as he exposed her to his gaze. Heat flushed her cheeks, but she did not dare to stop him. When his mouth covered her nipple, the shock of the sensation left her gasping.

"Christopher." Her voice trembled with pleasure as he lavished upon her.

"You're so damn beautiful." His words, a low growl that teased her flesh. His eyes met hers, the intensity in his gaze made her heart stutter. "I envy the man who wins your heart."

His words struck something deep within her, but she would only dwell on their meaning later. For now, she was lost in the feel of his hands and the fervent press of his lips.

When he finally pulled away, setting her gown to rights and helping her down from the table, she noted the faint marks of his stubble against her flushed skin. She would have to wear a fichu at dinner to avoid any awkward questions.

"I should not be kissing you or touching you so." He ran a hand through his hair, regret shadowing his eyes. "I ought to be horsewhipped for wanting you as I do."

"You've been honest with me, Christopher." Matilda slipped off the table and attempted to gain her wits. "I know you do not want marriage at this time. And I do not wish to marry a man who does not love me. But I also enjoy these interludes and hope they can continue while I remain at your parents' estate."

"But they cannot." He sighed, clearly pained.

Matilda met his eyes and tipped up her chin in defense. She did not wish for him to feel guilty. They were only having a little fun together. No one would get hurt by their arrangement, least of all her. "Let me decide for myself when we've taken our interludes too far, my lord. Surely, you know by now that I am the last woman in England who wishes to be told what is best for her, both in love and life. I enjoy my freedom and how you make me feel when we kiss. An innocent kiss does not mean that I will demand marriage from you. I promise you that."

His lips twitched into a faint smile. "That I do know. But it doesn't make this any less erroneous."

"And yet," she murmured, leaning up to press one last kiss to his lips, "never has it felt more right."

CHAPTER
TEN

Lord Charteris was unusually quiet that evening at dinner, speaking little to anyone at the table, unlike the lively conversations of nights before.

Matilda sat beside Charlotte, noticing her friend's furtive glances toward her brother and guest. Lord Charteris seemed reflective, perhaps rattled by the kiss they had shared earlier. Matilda couldn't help but wonder if he was more affected than he let on. Their stolen kisses while she'd been a guest here had been delightful, and she hoped they might continue before her departure. It was certainly a far more enjoyable way to pass the time than sitting embroidering all day, which she'd never been overly fond of.

"I think Lord and Lady Haverly wish for Christopher to marry their daughter, Lady Delphine," Charlotte whispered so no one else could hear. "I overheard them speaking with my parents earlier today. They didn't know I was in the library. I was seated in one of the wingback chairs facing the window, reading, and they came in discussing how Christopher and Lady Delphine are of age and ought to marry. They seem to believe them a most suitable match."

Matilda glanced across the table at Lady Delphine, who sat adjacent to Lord Charteris. The woman's gaze lingered on Christopher, her expression soft and admiring. Suspicion knotted Matilda's stomach, and she reached for her wine, the cool, ruby liquid fortifying her resolve not to care what Lord Charteris did, or Lady Delphine, for that matter.

While she enjoyed his mouth, that did not mean he would make a satisfying husband.

"Do you think your brother wishes for such a union?" Matilda stated, remembering their past conversations. "I, for one, have not seen him display any particular interest in Lady Delphine, though she's kind, pretty, and undeniably eligible." She paused. "I have heard your brother state he's not in the market for a wife just yet."

While unions were often arranged by the great families of the *ton*, she rarely saw love matches come out of such marriages. More often than not, the couple barely spent time together or showed any affection.

Suitability in the eyes of society was one thing, but she longed for something more—something her parents' marriage had lacked.

Love...

"I do not think so," Charlotte replied. "We

love Lady Delphine dearly, but Christopher is so often away. I believe the distance has kept their affections from deepening. But maybe in Lady Delphine's case, her heart grew stronger by the separation."

"Then I feel sorry for her if that is the case." Matilda glanced toward Christopher and found him watching her. He sipped his wine, his eyes burning a trail across the table, sending a delicious heat coursing through her. Heat kissed her cheeks, and she reached for her own wine glass for added fortification.

He was so handsome and impossibly magnetic. He took her breath away, and she longed for more—so many more stolen moments with him.

"Do you now think with certainty that Lady Delphine has remained unmarried in hopes of securing your brother's hand?" Matilda asked.

"I do," Charlotte said, popping a roasted potato into her mouth. "I think she's been waiting for him, but I fear she'll leave here as she always does—unmarried and ever closer to spinsterhood."

"But she's an heiress from a good family and stunningly beautiful. Why not return to London and find a husband there? She might find a love match, as you and Genevieve have."

"I suspect her heart is too set on Christopher." Charlotte sighed. "It's a tragedy. She's destined to be heartbroken."

"That is very unfortunate." Matilda forced

herself to look away from Christopher, lest anyone notice the interactions between them.

After several more courses, the main meal came to an end, and dessert was served—a decadent wine-flavored syllabub that melted on the tongue, its fruity acidity wholly balanced by the creamy texture.

They retired to the drawing room after not another bite could be had. The terrace doors stood open, allowing a gentle, jasmine-scented breeze to drift into the room, weaving its way through the air and bringing with it a refreshing touch of the evening's tranquility.

Lady Delphine took to the piano, playing a lively gavotte that soon had Charlotte and Lord Lacy moving to the side of the room to dance.

Lord Charteris approached Matilda, a playful grin on his lips putting her on guard. "May I have this dance, my lady?" He bowed before her, and she blinked in surprise. He did not seem the kind to seek attention from anyone so openly. But instead of questioning his reasons, she placed her hand in his and allowed him to guide her to join the others in what became an impromptu ball.

"I do not believe I've mentioned this yet, Lady Matilda," his words low and intimate, "but you look particularly beautiful this evening. I much prefer your hair loose like this rather than swept into the towering wigs so many ladies favor."

"Do you?" Her smile grew as he spun her gracefully within the dance. "I must admit, it's far more comfortable. And it means I can retire to bed much faster at the end of the night. Perhaps wigs will fall out of fashion someday, and we'll all wear our hair loose to balls, as I am now."

"I certainly hope so." His eyes dipped to her lips, and she couldn't help but wonder what he was thinking.

"I cannot stop thinking about our kiss this afternoon."

Butterflies swarmed in her stomach, left her longing for more. "It was enjoyable, was it not?" she teased. "And if you remain a charming gentleman this evening, I might reward you with another tomorrow."

"Tomorrow is too far away," he murmured.

For a fleeting moment, she considered indulging him, but they could not sneak away without arousing suspicion. Besides, Lady Delphine's obvious admiration for him weighed on her conscience.

"We cannot." She needed to remain strong. "Not that I don't wish to, but I think it would be cruel to ignore another's feelings."

His gaze flicked to Lady Delphine. His mouth tightened before he returned his attention to her. "I'll steal those kisses while I can before they're no longer mine to take."

Her breath caught. "For those kisses to be yours forever, you will have to make me fall in love with you—and marry me. Are you prepared to do that, my lord? I did not think you were in the market for a wife."

He grinned but did not deny it outright. A promising sign, perhaps? The dance ended, and he bowed, escorting her back to her seat. "Good evening, Lady Matilda," he said, striding toward where his parents stood with Lord and Lady Haverly.

Matilda's heart twisted as she watched him exchange words with his parents and guests. Lady Delphine joined them, and surprisingly, Lord Charteris offered his arm and led the young woman onto the terrace, out of sight.

Much to the delight of both their parents.

Unease prickled down her spine, and before she could stop herself, she wished everyone goodnight and retired for the evening. Alone in her chamber, she tried to convince herself it didn't matter what he did or with whom and that a stroll on the terrace with anyone did not mean anything.

But as she lay sleepless in the dark, a thought echoed endlessly.

Perhaps it did.

CHAPTER
ELEVEN

The carriage drive into the quaint town of Sevenoaks for the assembly ball took twenty minutes from the ducal estate. Outside, the rhythmic clatter of hooves echoed on the dry, stony road, and the warm glow of lanterns lit the way as they approached the town limits. The assembly rooms were stone structures with a thatch roof, and townspeople and carriages lined up to enjoy a night of revelry.

Inside, they were greeted by the local vicar and his wife, whose smiles were as practiced as their bows. The Duke and Duchess of D'Estel spent several minutes speaking to the local gentry and those in attendance, their polished manners drawing admiration. Then, as was their custom, they moved toward the side of the room to allow space for the more daring souls eager to dance.

Lord and Lady Haverly took to the floor,

joined by Lord Charteris and Lady Delphine. Matilda stood beside the duchess, her gloved hands clasped before her as she watched Christopher spin Lady Delphine about the ballroom floor with perfection. The man really knew how to dance and make even that pastime look effortless.

The lively strains of the violins and Christopher's low laugh carried above the chatter of the crowd. Together, he and Lady Delphine made a striking pair—elegant, poised, and undeniably well-matched. The sight sent an uncomfortable ripple down Matilda's spine.

Why did it matter to her whom he danced with? She did not wish for him to be her husband. He did not love and adore her as one's husband or potential suitor should. And he had not given her false hope that he was falling for her charms, even if his kisses were so very enjoyable.

Still, Matilda sighed, wishing it were she who was enjoying the floor with his lordship. Not that he had much choice regarding whom he danced with first. Lady Delphine and her parents had accompanied Lord Charteris to the ball. There was little doubt a conversation on who would accompany him on his first dance had been had in the carriage and, with it, his obligation to ask the young lady traveling with him.

Matilda stood observing the dancers just as a young man she did not recognize approached the Duke and Duchess D'Estel, bowing with impeccable grace. His dark hair was artfully styled, and his attire spoke of wealth. Her heart fluttered, for it seemed an introduction was imminent when Her Grace turned to find her in the crowd.

"Lady Matilda, my dear, come join us," Her Grace beckoned her to their side, and Matilda took a fortifying breath and pasted on a welcoming smile.

"My dear, may I introduce you to Mr. Melvin Lincoln of Thornhaven Abbey," the duchess said. "He resides not far from here and is eager to make your acquaintance."

"Mr. Lincoln, a pleasure to meet you." Matilda offered her hand, his fingers brushing over hers as he bowed. His mischievous gaze met hers when he straightened, sending a faint warmth to her cheeks.

"The pleasure is all mine, Lady Matilda," he replied, his voice rich and smooth. "If you would honor me with the next dance, I would be delighted."

"Of course, she's willing, sir," the duchess interjected with a smile that left no room for refusal.

Matilda nodded, suppressing a grin at the duchess's attempt at matchmaking. "I would honored, Mr. Lincoln, thank you."

As they moved toward the dance floor, Matilda caught Lord Charteris's gaze from across the room. His expression was inscrutable, but his lips pressed into a thin line, and something about his posture conveyed disapproval.

Ignoring him, she turned her attention back to her dance partner. "Does Thornhaven Abbey boast any ghosts?" she asked as they waited for the last dance to end and theirs to begin. "It sounds like the kind of place where ghouls abound."

His lips curved into a handsome smile. "Indeed, it does, my lady. Tales of spectral figures wandering the halls at night are whispered by the staff. Perhaps you would care to investigate for yourself? With your family, of course."

The violins struck up a lively tune, and Mr. Lincoln led her into the opening steps of the dance. The floor beneath her shoes felt smooth as they danced across it. The air was filled with the mingling scents of beeswax candles and rosewater perfume, and the rustle of fabric accompanied their movements like a second melody.

"Perhaps I shall," Matilda replied with a laugh. "I must admit, the idea intrigues me."

"Then you must join me for the winter ball I host before closing the Abbey for the Season," he suggested, his eyes twinkling. "It would be an honor to welcome you, your friends, and any family you wish to invite."

"That sounds delightful." Matilda grinned as the steps of the dance brought them closer. For a moment, the proximity felt almost intimate before they separated again in accordance with the steps.

The conversation flowed easily, and Matilda found herself thoroughly charmed.

"You're lucky I'm here this evening, Lady Matilda. I had an unfortunate event where my horse threw me only this morning, so I hope my dancing is to your standard. I must admit to feeling a little sore tonight."

Matilda's steps faltered as she took in his words. "Mr. Lincoln, I'm so sorry for you then, but I will say your dancing has not been harmed. In fact, you dance very well for a gentleman who is injured."

"You flatter me." He smiled.

Matilda laughed. "Maybe a little, but I'm also telling the truth." She paused. "How fortunate you are that you are only a little sore. A fall off a horse could have had a far more ominous outcome than missing a town assembly."

"Indeed," he agreed, his gaze softening. "For I would not have had the pleasure of meeting or dancing with you, Lady Matilda."

Her cheeks flushed, and she faltered in the dance for a moment. Recovering quickly, she glanced at the throng of guests and locked eyes with Lord Charteris. He stood alone, whisky in hand, watching her with something akin to vexation.

His jaw was set, his expression thunderous. Was he angry with her? She frowned and turned her attention back to Mr. Lincoln, confused as to why Lord Charteris was displeased. They were friends who shared kisses, nothing more. He had no reason to be put out by her dancing with another man. He knew she was looking for a love match, just as he was looking for no match.

As the dance came to an end, Mr. Lincoln bowed low. "Thank you, my lady. I hope this will not be the last time we meet, and please do consider coming to my ball. The Abbey is not far from here."

Matilda nodded in agreement. "I believe we'll meet again," she replied, hoping that may be true.

He escorted her back to the Duke and Duchess D'Estel, but Lord Charteris appeared at her side before she could say more. His presence was as commanding as his grip on her arm was.

"A turn about the room, if you please, Lady Matilda." He pulled her away without another word, and not wanting to cause a scene, she followed his lead.

He led her away, and she frowned. "Is something amiss?"

He did not answer immediately, instead steering her toward a quiet corner where potted plants hid them from view. "I did not realize your interests lay with an untitled country gentleman. He is wealthy, I will give him that, but the dress you're wearing this evening would be a trinket of the past. His purse is not deep enough to keep a duke's daughter clothed."

Matilda bristled. "Well, maybe I would remain naked in Mr. Lincoln's presence if he were my husband; therefore, it would not signify what I wore." She paused, taking a deep breath to calm her ire. "Mr. Lincoln is a gentleman in every sense of the word," she retorted. "I see no reason why you disparage him."

Christopher's gaze darkened. "I do not mock him, but you must see the absurdity. Your father would never allow such a match."

She lifted her chin, wanting to cast out his words. "Perhaps he would if I cared for Mr. Lincoln."

"You're deluding yourself," he snapped, though his gaze drifted to her lips. "And yet, for all your stubbornness, there is something irresistible about you. I can see why Mr. Lincoln sought you out."

Her breath caught, heat blooming in her cheeks. "You lie. You have not sought me out once this evening, only now to berate me like a child."

"I am merely trying to make you see sense," he murmured. "You are beautiful, though you are also insufferable and perhaps a little desperate to find love."

Matilda laughed, the sound void of humor. "High praise indeed." She stepped back, placing much-needed distance between them. "But perhaps you ought to be more concerned about your own life, my lord. By singling out Lady Delphine this evening as you have, they will soon expect an offer of marriage. What a shame it is that you do not want a wife. She would dote on you, I'm sure."

She turned on her heel and returned to the

Duchess, leaving Lord Charteris alone. A faint smile graced her lips as she weaved through the crowd. The sight of his lordship's shocked expression was satisfying—a fitting repayment for his sharp words, though they had wounded her more deeply than she cared to admit.

CHAPTER
TWELVE

As the notes of a pianoforte began to play, Christopher bowed before Lady Matilda and then escorted her onto the dance floor. The impatience to have her in his arms again was beyond his comprehension.

The sight of her turning her back to him, returning to his parents as if their conversation was at an end, would never do.

What was happening to him? What was it about Matilda that left him all at sixes and sevens? And what the devil would he do about Lady Delphine?

That she continued to believe they ought to be married and insisted on announcing the long-ago betrothal he'd offered when they were but children was outrageous.

That she wished to hold him to such a foolish promise was beyond comprehension. He did not know how to tell her their marriage could not be

—too much time had passed. A childhood infatuation had long since turned into nothing more than friendship.

But Matilda was another matter entirely.

She unknowingly had bewitched him. Around her, he couldn't think straight and often found himself wanting to say more in her company, but unable to do so. Had his tongue somehow lost its ability to form words? And his annoyance at seeing her with Mr. Lincoln had ended with him chastising her instead of kissing her as he'd wanted.

None of the feelings that coursed through his blood matched his character. He was an independent and confident gentleman, a future duke, not a man who became jealous of a woman's suitors.

Matilda slipped into his arms, her slender form fitting against his like a glove. He could not help but reflect on his earlier remarks when they'd first met. He might not have been looking for a wife then, but she had certainly caught his attention now. He could see himself quite happily married to her.

His gaze drifted over the sea of elegantly coiffed heads. Across the assembly room, Lady Delphine watched them, disappointment clouding her eyes, and Christopher knew he needed to repair the damage his childhood folly had caused.

Lady Delphine deserved love and happiness. However, he was not the man to give her that, and it was time she discovered someone who could.

"I thought our conversation was over for this evening, Lord Charteris. You're quite the popular gentleman this evening. So many ladies vying for your hand, you did not have to dance with me out of duty." Matilda looked up at him, a mischievous twist to her full lips. Lips that had kept him sleepless since the day they had met. Lips he knew were soft when kissed—pliable, yielding, and wanton when required to be so.

Lips he wanted to kiss again.

He watched her as they danced, drinking in her pretty features. Her hair was swept up into a fashionable chignon adorned with pearls, her lips painted a delicate rose pink, and her diamond earrings swayed with every step.

A fist clenched in his stomach at how stunningly beautiful she was. Beautiful enough to make him—and many other gentlemen this evening—lose their minds and sensibilities.

"As the future Duke of D'Estel, it is my duty to dance with as many ladies as propriety demands," he replied. "I will oversee this county one day, after all, and I want to be known as affable and approachable."

"Oh, I have not forgotten. And perhaps, if I can secure Mr. Lincoln's affections, we shall live nearby."

Christopher cleared his throat and bit down the sharp retort that rose in his throat. "I do not wish to quarrel with you, nor do I like how our previous conversation ended, but I still do not think that would be wise, Lady Matilda."

"No?" she queried, raising her brow and looking at him expectantly. "And why not? We're friends, and I'm an old friend of your family. There is nothing wrong with us becoming neighbors."

"There is something very wrong with that notion."

He did not wish to spell it out or alarm her, yet the truth—his secret sentiments—gnawed at him. Her being married might offer her some protection from him, but he doubted that would keep his longings at bay for long.

As treacherous and ungentlemanly as it seemed, something about Lady Matilda made him not care about the pain he could cause others, so long as he could have her.

"Why?" she asked, puzzled.

"Because." He swept her close through a turn in the dance. "I would want you even more if I were not married to you. Knowing you belonged to another would drive me to distraction. I do not think I could resist stealing a kiss or two or pressing you for more."

"More?" She bit her lip, her eyes growing heavy with understanding, even though her following words were contradictory to her expression. "Whatever do you mean?"

He ground his teeth, reluctant to say more. But she had asked.

"As a married woman, I would have no

qualms in cuckolding your husband if it meant I could have you in my bed."

Her mouth opened and closed several times before she let out an awkward chuckle. "You did not just say that, my lord."

He stared into her dark-blue eyes, ensuring she understood every word he spoke. "I mean everything I communicate, always. Should you find love—or at least contentment—in marriage to another, and you live nearby, there is every chance I would still want you. I enjoy our kisses. And nothing within me doubts that more than kisses would also be satisfying."

"But I could grow heavy with a child should I act so recklessly. You could be forced to watch me bear your child with another man. That your possible heir could carry another name. And you believe you would be all right with that? I think not."

The idea had not occurred to him before she mentioned it. Her words painted the outcome with painful clarity. A gut-wrenching twist of jealousy told him he could not stomach such a reality.

"You are correct. I would not like that," he admitted.

"Well then, you'll have to marry me, and that would not happen." She threw him a smile that left him breathless, and he laughed, hoping only a little that she was teasing.

"But I thought we were merely enjoying each

other's kisses for now. Turning such little interludes into serious commitment seems rather hasty."

She shrugged, glancing away to study the other dancers crowding about them. "I would not stray from my marriage bed, Lord Charteris, even for you and your sweet kisses."

"So you would be lost to me." He narrowed his eyes, willing her to look at him again, to focus only on him.

"I would. And it would be for the best. I would hate for you to cause a scandal merely because you could not ask me to be your wife when you had the chance. Now," she said, meeting his eyes, "I know you expressed you're not looking for a wife. But if it's just that you've not found the right woman, do not discard me so easily. I may be the one who got away, and then you'll have to live with the disappointment for the rest of your life. And how sad for us both if that were to occur."

He did not reply, but her words settled deep within his soul, and he could feel the heavy truth about what she had spoken.

"We do get along well, and there is passion between us. Why, even now, in your arms before these guests, all I can think about is how much I want to be alone with you. I want your hands on me. Wanton behavior for a well-bred young woman? Yes, but I do not care when it comes to you."

He shook his head, drowning in a pool of need with no desire to surface.

"I want to be alone with you, too." And before the end of the evening, he would ensure they were.

CHAPTER
THIRTEEN

The evening ended with a delightful and invigorating cotillion before everyone in attendance began to bid their goodnights by either walking home or waiting for their carriages to arrive.

Matilda stood with Charlotte and Lord Lacy, the wind gaining in strength since their arrival several hours ago. A distinct smell of rain hung in the air, heavy and foreboding, but also welcome after the horrendous heat they'd been suffering through.

"I do hope we can arrive home before the weather breaks." No sooner had Charlotte uttered those fateful words than the heavens opened and drenched everyone unlucky enough to be outside still.

Matilda darted back into the hall, shaking droplets from her damp gown. The rich scent of rain-soaked muslin and perfume greeted her as the other guests crowded in to avoid the downpour. She spotted Lord Charteris speaking to the local vicar, blissfully unaware of the commotion outside.

Several carriages came and went, and in the haste to escape the dreadful weather, Matilda missed securing a spot in the carriage with Charlotte.

Just as she was about to run outside to catch Lord and Lady Haverly's carriage back to the estate, an arm wrapped firmly around her waist, halting her steps.

"You can ride back to the house with me."

The feel of Christopher's strong arm and chiseled abdomen pressing against her back left her wits momentarily scattered. She pushed down her response to him and fought to control her racing heart. "I can't possibly," she argued, stepping out of his hold. Glancing around, she sighed, thankful no one had seen his familiarity.

"Well, you cannot stay here." He gestured to the dwindling guests and the nearly empty roadway before the assembly rooms, where only a handful of carriages remained. "I rode my horse in but have a carriage to return home. I'd planned to stop at the local tavern for a beer or two, but I can return you home before heading out again."

Matilda narrowed her eyes, unsure she liked the idea of Lord Charteris going out at night. Alone... "A tavern? Do you often frequent such establishments, my lord?" She didn't know why, but the idea of him lingering in taverns late into the night left her oddly unsettled. What did he get up to in such places? Did she even want to know?

No, her thoughts immediately answered, *especially if it involved the fairer sex gracing his bed at the end of the evening.*

"There's nothing wrong with sharing a friendly drink with the locals, Lady Matilda. Do not act so high and mighty—it doesn't suit you."

"I was not acting high and mighty. I'd have no issue drinking with anyone if I were invited."

"Then why do you wish for me not to go?" He raised a knowing brow, and she lifted her chin, refusing to play his game or tell him she might envy anyone who spent time with his lordship.

She did not respond, and after a heartbeat or two, he smiled.

"Do you wish to come along?" The sincerity in his question bolstered her resolve to accept his invitation.

"If you think it would not jeopardize my reputation by entering such an establishment."

"Well, it could, I won't lie. But if we remove that ridiculous wig and your jewelry and lose that fine lace fichu, I think we could pass you off as someone whose fortune lies in...other ventures."

A blush heated her cheeks knowing what he meant by that. "I think I would enjoy a beer or two at the tavern. I've never been and would like to see how others spend their evenings."

Lord Charteris gestured toward one of the remaining carriages outside, and they ran through the puddle-strewn courtyard before climbing inside. The interior smelled of damp leather and wood polish used to keep it pristine.

Matilda reached for her necklace, but the clasp refused to budge. She turned her back to Christopher. "Will you undo my necklace? I can't seem to manage it."

"Of course." Christopher cleared his throat before he reached for her. Cool, calloused fingers brushed her neck, sending an unexpected shiver down her spine. She closed her eyes, the carriage rolling toward the tavern, and felt his warm breath against her skin as he worked the clasp.

The necklace gave way, and he reached over her shoulder, holding it out. "Here you are."

She opened her reticule and slipped it inside, removing her earrings as well.

"Will you also help me unpin my hair," she asked, looking back at him over her shoulder. "I'm not wearing a large wig tonight, so it shouldn't take long." Her hair was already disheveled from the downpour, strands falling loose from the pins.

She worked at the front while Christopher removed pins from the back. Again, his touch sent her pulse racing. The occasional brush of his fingers against her scalp left her breathless. Why did she react to him this way? She wasn't in love with him—she knew that. But there was no denying she was very much in lust with him.

"I think I have them all." He handed her the pins, and she placed them with her jewelry before removing the wig. Running her fingers through her damp hair, she tried to smooth it into something less disheveled.

"How do I look, my lord?" Matilda turned to face him. Christopher seemed larger, more imposing, and devastatingly handsome in the shadowy carriage.

The storm had drenched his hair too, leaving it unkempt, as though he'd just stepped from a bath or ran his fingers through it. Her heart pounded, and a knot of need burned in her stomach for the man before her.

Dear Lord, get a hold of yourself, Matilda. You're behaving like a wanton.

He reached up, tucking a lock of her hair behind her ear. His fingers grazed her lobe as he pulled away. "Beautiful as always. But you don't need me to convey that, do you? You already know."

His compliment sent a rush of warmth through her chest. The longing in his eyes made her want to abandon all propriety and savor this moment.

She reached up, fingers brushing his damp curls. "As are you, my lord, though I suspect you already know that too."

A wicked grin curved his lips as the carriage rocked to a halt before the tavern.

Matilda leaned toward the window. The White Hart was alive with activity, patrons coming and going, and many from the assembly room ball sought refuge in the foyer.

The driver opened the door, and Lord Charteris leaped out, turning to help her down. "Watch the carriage, John. We've left valuables inside. We won't be long."

"Right you are, my lord."

Matilda followed his lordship inside. The air was thick with the scent of ale, pipe smoke, and damp wool. They pushed through the lively crowd to the bar, where Lord Charteris ordered two beers.

"Have you ever tasted ale before?" he asked, passing her a tankard.

Matilda shook her head, smelling the drink. She winced, unsure she liked the earthy, bitter scent. Hesitantly, she sipped.

"It's not my preferred beverage," she admitted, wrinkling her nose, "but it'll do well enough."

He chuckled, the deep sound sending a flutter through her chest.

"Why are you so likable?" she asked, narrowing her eyes. "When we first met, I thought you much changed from the boy I knew, but the man you've become has grown on me."

"So, you like me now?" His smirk made her want to laugh.

She shrugged. "I do. More than I ought."

"Don't fall in love with me, Lady Matilda. I'll break your heart," he warned, a shadow passing over his expression before quickly masking it.

But she had seen it and knew his words rang true. But could she change his mind? Could he fall in love with her instead of remaining a bachelor? Surely, a loving wife to warm one's bed was much better than remaining alone and having endless lovers that one couldn't remember their names a day later.

"Not if I break yours first," she teased, wanting to keep the evening light and uncomplicated.

"Touche." He clinked their glasses together. "Now drink. This is the first of many ales I want you to try before we return you home."

She could toast and drink to that.

CHAPTER
FOURTEEN

Several hours later, Matilda stumbled into the carriage, her gown catching on the step. A loud tearing sound followed, and she winced. Her maid would undoubtedly be furious with her in the morning with whatever damage she had done to her attire.

Lord Charteris laughed, leaning down to help her gather the gown before he climbed into the carriage and settled across from her.

The sight of him blurred, possibly a result of far-too-many ales she had consumed. Matilda had discovered, much to her dismay, that the more she drank, the less offensive the brew tasted. Now, as the carriage lurched forward and they began the journey back to the ducal estate, regret settled heavily in her stomach alongside the liquor.

"Oh dear." She pressed a hand to her forehead. She would never survive the ride home if the carriage continued to spin around her.

Lord Charteris leaned toward the carriage door and slid the window open, allowing a cooling breeze to flow inside. The night air carried the scent of rain-soaked earth and the distant aroma of smoke from the village chimneys.

"Thank you." Matilda closed her eyes as the fresh air kissed her flushed cheeks. "I feel I may need this to survive the journey home."

"I thought as much," he replied. He turned to look out the window, a faint frown creasing his brow. "I shouldn't have kept you out so late. I imagine there will be words exchanged when we return."

Matilda cringed at the thought of a scolding and hoped it wouldn't come to that. The night had been so delightful, filled with laughter and a sense of freedom she rarely experienced. She didn't want it marred by reproach.

"Well," she said with a small, lopsided smile, "we shall face such consequences when they come. I'm far too foxed to care what anyone might say."

His warm and rich laughter filled the carriage, making her heart flutter, and her stomach tighten. She'd been uncharacteristically tactile with him tonight, leaning on him, touching his arm, basking in his presence. She couldn't help it—he was a safer haven in the bustling tavern than anyone else, yet she hadn't been able to ignore the hardened muscles beneath his clothes or how his laughter seemed to vibrate through her.

He was a handsome man, and she could no longer deny how much she liked him.

Wanted him.

For herself...

Why couldn't she make the man sitting across from her fall in love with her? He didn't seem to mind her stepping outside the strictures of her sex or the rigid expectations of society. If anything, he seemed to admire her boldness, her unwillingness to let others clip her wings.

He had become one of her favorite people—outside Charlotte and Genevieve. How could she not fall for a man of such quality?

"That's certainly true." He ran a hand through his disheveled hair. "And I must admit, I'm just as foxed as you are. At this point, I cannot bring myself to care about the setdowns we're about to face."

The motion of his arm caught her attention, and her gaze lingered on the way his shirt stretched over the muscles of his forearm. Her breath hitched, and when their eyes met, the air in the carriage seemed to change—thicken with unspoken tension.

"You shouldn't look at me like that, Lady Matilda," he warned, his voice low and rough. "You'll make me act in an ungentlemanly-like manner, and then we'll both regret it."

Her lips twitched into a teasing smile. "Sounds intriguing, my lord. Perhaps you could explain what this ungentlemanly-like behavior entails?"

He closed his eyes briefly, a soft groan escaping him. Then, wagging a finger before him, he replied, "Behave, my lady, for God knows I will not if you do not want me to."

She raised her brow, her skin prickling with awareness. "Who is to know if we misbehave in the carriage?" she countered, a mischievous fire simmering inside her. "You haven't kissed me in days, and I find myself in need of such indulgences. What lady doesn't enjoy such treats?"

"You want me to kiss you?" His brows lifted in mock surprise. "Here, in the carriage?"

"Why not?" She glanced around the dimly lit interior. "No one is here to see us. And besides, I've never kissed a man while foxed. It might be... enlightening."

"Unlikely." He chuckled, his tone edged with humor. "But I am more than happy to oblige a friend."

He moved to sit beside her, and Matilda wasted no time slipping her arms around his neck. She tilted her face up to his, her gaze softening as she drank in the details of his features—the sharp line of his jaw, the slight curve of his lips, the way his eyes darkened with intent.

"Then kiss me, *friend*..." she murmured in a sultry whisper she hoped was alluring.

He closed the distance between them. His lips captured hers in a kiss that was both possessive and tender.

His arms encircled her waist, drawing her closer until her chest pressed firmly against his.

The heat of his body, the strength in his embrace, and the rhythmic thrum of his heart sent a shiver of longing through her.

Matilda kissed him back, parting her lips to deepen the connection. His low moan vibrated against her, and the sound only spurred her on. Her hands tangled in his hair, her fingers threading through the damp curls as their kiss grew more fervent.

She wanted more—so much more.

Without thinking, she shifted, kneeling on the seat to straddle his lap. He made no move to stop her. Instead, his hands slid down her back, cupping her bottom to press her closer.

She gasped, breaking the kiss for only a moment before capturing his lips once again. Even through the voluminous fabric of her skirts, she could feel his arousal teasing her into a fever.

Her hips moved instinctively, rolling against him in a rhythm that made her dizzy with pleasure. The ache building within her was unlike anything she had ever felt—intense, consuming, and utterly irresistible.

"Matilda," he groaned, as his hands gripped her hips, guiding her movements. "I need to feel you."

She helped him push aside her gown, their hands fumbling in desperation. When the fabric no longer separated them, the warmth of his hands on her thighs sent a jolt of bliss through her.

The sensations grew sharper, more intoxicating with each roll of her hips and teasing of his hands. She was on the precipice of something incredible, something she had only ever experienced in the privacy of her room.

A wave of pleasure crashed over her, and she trembled in the aftermath, her breath coming in soft, ragged gasps. "Christopher," she moaned, her lips brushing against his as she murmured his name.

He shuddered beneath her, his grip tightening as he buried his face in her neck. "Matilda," he rasped, the words thick with emotion. "I've never... That is to say..." He trailed off, catching his breath before continuing. "That was very pleasant indeed."

She chuckled, running her fingers through his hair as she kissed his forehead. "Indeed," she echoed his response.

"I fear I'll desire more carriage interludes now," he admitted, a wry smile tugging at his lips.

She grinned, leaning in to kiss him again—quick and sweet. "I fear I shall as well."

CHAPTER
FIFTEEN

Christopher sat at the breakfast table the following morning, breaking his fast. He was ravenous, devouring the ham and eggs the cook had served, yet his appetite for the woman seated across from him far exceeded any hunger for food.

Lady Matilda. Innocent, sweet, and the very picture of propriety—if one didn't know better.

But he did. Oh, he knew better.

After their escapades the previous evening in the local village tavern and then the carriage, he now fully understood what Lady Matilda was capable of. She had awakened emotions within him he had long thought himself immune to.

He liked her—more than he ought to, given his steadfast determination to remain a bachelor. Or the fact that he'd proposed to a lady in his youth who was determined to hold him to that arrangement.

"Oh, I do hope this summer storm passes

soon," Lady Delphine remarked, her delicate fingers tracing the rim of the teacup. "I planned to walk the grounds today. I need to stretch my legs after that delightful supper I consumed last night."

"Indeed, I shall join you," Charlotte chimed in. "A brisk walk through the gardens would suit me well, too."

Christopher focused on his plate of food, intent on avoiding the conversation, lest he be roped into their plans. The last thing he wanted was to stroll through the gardens, forced into idle chatter with Lady Delphine—a situation he was determined to avoid until he could make her see sense regarding their youthful engagement, a promise he no longer intended to honor.

After last night in the carriage with Matilda, he could not honor the promise without sabotaging the possibility of a happy marriage with another woman.

A woman he cared for more than he'd thought possible.

"I did not see you return last evening, brother." Charlotte's tone was casual, but her gaze sharp. "Was there an issue with the carriage after we left?"

Her question caught him off guard, and without thinking, he glanced at Matilda, who was staring at him. Her large, blue eyes wide with concern.

"A delay in leaving, I'm afraid. Several revelers waylaid me, and Lady Matilda and I arrived a little later than the rest of you. You were all abed by the time we returned."

"Yes, it was a tiring night, and we did not stay up," Lady Delphine interjected, her eyes narrowing as her gaze flicked to Matilda, unmistakably cool.

Christopher stiffened. Something about the way Delphine glowered at Matilda left him uneasy. Had she seen their return? Other than the footman at the door, the household had been quiet when they arrived. The family, he had assumed, was asleep.

Had he been wrong that they all were abed?

Had Lady Delphine remained up, watching from the shadows? Had she witnessed the kiss he had stolen from Matilda on the staircase? Did she know how much restraint it had taken not to follow Matilda to her room and make her his before he was free to do so?

He set down his cutlery and took a long sip of coffee, hoping to mask his discomfort. Hell, he prayed that wasn't the case. He needed to resolve things with Lady Delphine before he could even entertain the idea of offering for Matilda.

He frowned. Suppose he offered to her at all. Their shared friendship may not be enough for Lady Matilda to commit to him. After all, she wanted a love match, and while he liked her very much, he was unsure his feelings were deep enough to equal love.

"Would you like to join us for our walk, Lord Charteris?" Lady Delphine asked, her smile soft but expectant. "I'm sure your sister wouldn't mind."

He smiled politely, dabbing his lips with his napkin before placing it neatly on the table. "I'm afraid I cannot this morning. I have much work to catch up on, including correspondence from Father's northern estate."

Pushing back his chair, he rose. "Good morning to you all."

With that, he left the room, relieved to have avoided further interaction with Lady Delphine. Not that he disliked her, on the contrary. She was a charming woman, suitable for many as a wife. But she stirred no fire in him, no desire.

Unlike Matilda.

Matilda made him feel alive in ways he hadn't experienced in years. Scotland had been a lonely exile, devoid of feminine company for much of the time. He'd grown resigned to solitude, assuming no woman could awaken his passion, so he'd become content with the idea of remaining a bachelor. Yet Matilda had proved him wrong with wit, daring, and intoxicating kisses.

Reaching his office, he closed the door and immersed himself in work. Letters from the steward, tenant issues, and estate repairs occupied him for many hours. Lunch passed unnoticed, and it wasn't until the clock chimed two that he leaned back in his chair and stretched, the first respite of the day.

The door creaked open, and there she was—

Lady Matilda. Her face lit with a warm smile, her presence as welcome as a burst of sunlight through storm clouds.

"I noticed you missed lunch." She stepped inside and closed the door behind her. He glanced at the plate of food she carried, and his stomach rumbled. "I thought you might like something to eat."

She walked toward him, the soft rustle of her skirts brushing against the polished floor. He watched the sway of her hips, unable to stop his body's immediate response to her presence.

He had been hungry, but was now ravenous for something entirely different. "Thank you," he said. "That is most kind. I completely lost track of time."

"I thought as much." She placed the plate on his desk, the aroma of baked potatoes and roasted meat wafting up to him. His stomach growled audibly, making her laugh.

"Oh dear, you are hungry!" she teased. Picking up a fork, she speared a piece of potato and held it to him. "Here, let me feed you, my lord."

Her tone was playful, but her eyes glinted with mischief. He held her gaze, reading the temptation there, and decided to play along. He opened his mouth, allowing her to slip the fork between his lips.

The potato was warm, buttery, and seasoned well. "Delicious." He watched to see her reaction to his words. Matilda leaned against the desk, observing him eat with a far too knowing expression. Then, without warning, she leaned down and pressed her lips to his.

The kiss was brief, but enough to make him lose his senses. Her tongue teased his, her lips soft and yielding. She pulled back with a sly smile, biting her bottom lip.

"Yes," she murmured seductively. "You're right—the potatoes are delicious."

A shiver ran down his spine, and he was utterly speechless for a moment. The control he had been fighting to maintain shattered.

He stood, scooping her up and setting her on the desk. The plate rattled precariously to her side, but he paid it no mind.

Reaching for the hem of her gown, he pushed it up over her hips, baring her to him. His hands gripped her thighs, pulling her hard against his arousal.

"You like teasing me, Lady Matilda?" he growled, his voice rough with desire.

She didn't flinch or shy away. Instead, she met his gaze with boldness, her cheeks flushed, and her lips parted.

"Who says I'm teasing?" Her hand slipped between them, and he stilled, his breath catching as her fingers found his manhood.

He gasped, his composure shattering to the winds. Her nimble fingers worked the buttons of his breeches, freeing him with a confidence that both startled and excited him.

"We cannot," he groaned, though his body betrayed him, pressing into her touch.

She removed her hand, but only to urge him closer. The heat of her bare skin against him was maddening, and when she shifted, guiding him between her folds, he nearly lost himself.

"I want you, Christopher." Her body trembled with need and there was only one way she could be satisfied. "I ached all night for you."

Her hips rocked against him, and he swore under his breath. He was so close to taking her and crossing a line from which there would be no return.

He pulled back just enough to look at her. She lay before him, open and glistening with arousal, her body a vision of temptation.

He stepped back and kneeled, his lips brushing against her inner thigh. He could not have her completely, but he could give her pleasure in other ways.

And he would sate the hunger within him.

With her.

CHAPTER
SIXTEEN

He stared at Matilda's glistening core, his mouth watering at the sight of her wanton, needy sex. She squirmed on his desk, perhaps anticipating what he was about to do.

And by God, he would enjoy making a meal of her...

Christopher slid his fingers along her slick folds, dipping one into her wetness before bringing it to his lips. He suckled his finger clean, savoring her curt but delicious taste.

Her eyes widened, and she bit her lip, watching him under a hooded gaze that mirrored all he felt in this moment—need, possession, excitement, and raw, unbridled lust.

His body burned. Every nerve was taut, his cock straining painfully against the confines of his breeches. He longed to free himself, press into her tight warmth, and claim her wholly.

"You like my touch." The words not a question but a statement of undeniable truth. She nodded, her thighs parting wider, inviting him to revel in her.

He pulled his chair closer and reached beneath her knees, drawing her toward him until she was positioned at the desk's edge. His lips quirked in a predatory smile as he dipped his head, his breath hot against her delicate folds.

The first touch of his tongue sent her hips bucking, her taste tangy and intoxicating. "I want you, Christopher," she beseeched, her fingers gripping the edge of the desk.

He smirked, determined to make her want him as fiercely as he wanted her. He wouldn't ruin her—he told himself this with resolve—but by God, he would ruin her for any other man. He intended to leave her wanting, aching for him and no one else.

Her legs rested on his shoulders as he lavished attention on her most sensitive place. His tongue teased her swollen nub, his lips sealing around it and suckling gently. Her moans filled the room, mingling with the rhythmic creak of the desk beneath her.

"I'm going to make you come so hard, Matilda," he murmured against her slickness. A promise he intended to keep.

She moaned his name, her hand slipping into his hair, fisting it as if to anchor herself to him. He welcomed her control, his mouth working tirelessly to bring her closer to the edge.

He brought two fingers to her mouth,

watching as she parted her lips and licked them with her tongue. The sight sent a fresh wave of heat coursing through his veins.

"I'm going to fuck you with my fingers." A promise he would fulfil. "And you're going to like it, but be discreet, like the proper lady I know you are."

She nodded, her intense gaze never leaving his. He pressed his fingers slowly inside her, relishing the way her body clenched around him.

"Christopher," she gasped, her hips lifting to meet his hand. Her body moved instinctively, her unspoken need guiding her movements.

"Shoosh, Matilda, don't make any noise." He paused, teasing her some more. "Suppose it were me filling you right now," he rasped, his mind a haze of right and wrong, temptation warring against what he wanted. "Hard and slow, filling you, teasing you until you beg me for release."

She whimpered, unable to form coherent words as his fingers found the spot within her that made her arch. She moaned, and he dipped his head, his tongue returning to her nubbin as he matched his strokes with flicks of his tongue.

"Harder, Christopher," she pleaded. "I need… I need you…"

Her words nearly broke his control. She was a duke's daughter, his equal in station and dignity. He couldn't take her maidenhead—not like this. Not yet.

But she was so close, her moans becoming

desperate, her body trembling beneath his touch. He couldn't stop now.

He stood, unbuttoning his breeches with one hand while the other held her firmly in place. His cock, thick and rigid, sprang free. He pulled her closer, the heat of her sex tantalizingly close to his.

"I want you inside me," she begged. "Please, Christopher. Do as I ask."

"I cannot." His words were pained, his jaw tight with restraint. He wouldn't take everything from her, no matter how desperately they wanted it. He still had some shred of morality left, even if it teetered on the brink of collapse.

"This will have to do," he said, positioning himself.

He rubbed the tip of his cock against her folds, their mingled arousal easing the glide. Her hands gripped the desk as she began to move with him, her body meeting his every motion.

She gasped, the friction sending them both spiraling. His heart thundered in his chest as he watched her unravel, her flushed cheeks and parted lips a vision of pure desire.

Her movements quickened, her cries becoming louder as her release neared. He matched her rhythm, forgetting the need for them to be quiet. His climax built, and he fought to hold on, to savor every second of this bewitched moment.

The sound of voices in the hall shattered their shared haze of pleasure.

Christopher froze, his head snapping toward

the door. Panic surged through him as he pulled back, swiftly fastening his breeches. With desperate efficiency, he pulled Matilda from the desk and adjusted her skirts and appearance just as the door swung open to reveal his parents.

His father joined them first, followed by his mother, whose narrowed eyes darted suspiciously between them.

"Ah, Lady Matilda," his father began, his tone genial but laced with curiosity. "I see you've been a dutiful friend, bringing Christopher his lunch. I trust you enjoyed your meal, my boy?"

Christopher, seated at his desk, inclined his head. "I enjoyed it very much," he replied steadily. His gaze met Matilda's briefly, a flicker of shared understanding passing between them. "Lady Matilda was just leaving. Thank you again for the delicious meal. I look forward to finishing it later."

Matilda's cheeks turned crimson, her composure visibly shaken. She nodded stiffly and turned toward the door. "Have a good afternoon," she murmured before slipping from the room without another word.

Christopher caught the knowing gleam in his mother's eyes and schooled his features into an impassive mask. The last thing he needed was for her to speculate further—or worse, intervene.

"We came to see if you would take Lady Delphine out in the carriage tomorrow," his father, oblivious to the tension in the room stated, as he ambled about. "She mentioned at lunch that it's been years since she visited the grotto near the river on the western side of the property. You enjoyed the place as a child, and I thought you might show her again."

Christopher leaned back in his chair, rubbing the back of his neck. "I'd prefer not." A headache formed behind his eyes. "I have no desire to give her—or anyone else—the impression that I'm courting her. We're friends, and that is all we shall remain."

His mother raised an eyebrow. "It would merely be a kindness, my dear son. Unless, of course, you'd rather take Lady Matilda. You seem quite the companions these days."

His gaze hardened, daring her to continue. She held his stare for a moment before relenting. "In any case," his mother smoothed out her skirts, attempting to ignore his words, "perhaps you could make it a group outing. Lady Matilda, Charlotte, and Lord Lacy might join you. That way, there would be no misunderstanding."

"That would be preferable," Christopher agreed. "I'll mention it at dinner this evening."

"Very good." His mother's gaze lingered on him, her lips curving into a faint smile. "And do freshen up before dinner, my dear. Your hair is askew."

He fought the urge to tame his hair, choosing instead to shrug. "Of course," he replied without inflection.

When the door finally closed behind them, Christopher exhaled in relief. Leaning back in his chair, he ran a hand through his hair, only to feel it sticking up in several places.

Damn it all to hell. What had they seen? What had they detected?

A sinking feeling told him his mother suspected far more than she let on. And if that were true, it was a development he neither wanted nor needed. He had enough on his plate as it was.

CHAPTER
SEVENTEEN

Matilda stumbled out of Christopher's office, her body afire—uncomfortable, unsatisfied, and aching for fulfillment that had been so cruelly denied.

Reaching the grand staircase, she clutched the polished wooden railing for support, her breath shaky, her thoughts scattered. She needed to regain some semblance of calm, though it seemed an impossible task. Not when her body still tingled with the promises Christopher's wicked mouth had whispered through every touch.

She covered her mouth with her hand to stem a frustrated curse. She would never be the same again after this afternoon, and nor did she wish to be.

Her cheeks flamed red when two maids passed and threw her a curious glance. She straightened and started up the stairs, desperate for the sanctuary of her room. She craved privacy—a quiet place to quell the fire raging inside her.

Thankfully, the corridor was empty, and she reached her room without encountering anyone else. Closing the door behind her, she leaned against it for a moment, her hand pressed to her chest as if to contain the erratic pounding of her heart.

She rang for her maid. A bath, she decided, would soothe her restless thoughts and wash away the lingering traces of Christopher's touch—not that she could ever truly erase the memory of his hands, his tongue, or the sinful way his lips had teased her.

A shiver ran down her spine.

Dear God, he was wicked. And she adored being wicked with him.

Her maid arrived promptly, thankfully distracting Matilda a little from her thoughts. "Please have a bath brought up immediately. And have my jasmine soap laid out. I wish to use that scent today." She walked to her dressing table and sat to remove the pins from her disheveled hair.

"Of course, Lady Matilda. I'll see to it at once."

Though it was unusual to bathe in the afternoon—especially since she hadn't been out riding or walking—a bath would help her feel refreshed for the evening.

Duchess D'Estel had mentioned dinner this evening would include the local reverend and his new wife. The prospect of polite conversation should have been welcome, yet all Matilda could think of was Christopher—his burning gaze, the way his fingers had coaxed pleasure from her, the promises left unfulfilled.

By the time the bath was prepared, steaming buckets of water carried in by sturdy footmen, Matilda's heart had settled into a normal rhythm. Her maid added a few drops of fragrant oil and placed soft towels on a nearby chair.

"Will there be anything else, my lady? Do you require assistance bathing?"

"No, thank you. I'll ring when I need help dressing for dinner."

"Very well, my lady."

Left alone, Matilda quickly shuffled out of her dress, which her maid had helped loosen, and stepped into the bath, the jasmine-scented water embracing her in soothing warmth. The sunlight streaming through the window bathed her skin in a golden glow, and she sighed, leaning back and letting her tension ebb away.

Outside, the gardens stretched toward the lake, their orderly beauty a sharp contrast to the chaos in her heart. She closed her eyes, but the image of Christopher's smoldering expression rose unbidden in her mind.

Her skin prickled with heat, her body remembering the delicious torment of his touch. Without shame, her hand slid between her thighs, her fingers mimicking the way he had teased her. She gasped, her movements tentative but growing bolder with every flick of the tender nub that ached for release.

Her imagination conjured him: his dark eyes fixed on hers as he knelt between her legs, his tongue tasting her, his lips caressing her most sensitive flesh. She moaned, her back arching against the porcelain.

"Christopher." His name, scarcely audible.

She imagined the feel of his manhood pressing against her, the way he had teased her so mercilessly, so achingly close to giving her everything. If only she had taken him fully...

Her climax washed over her in waves, her body trembling with the intensity of it. She gripped the tub's sides, her breath shallow as the euphoria ebbed, leaving her spent yet longing for the man who had ignited such passion.

Her gaze drifted to the window, and movement in the garden caught her eye. Leaning forward, she spotted Christopher strolling across the manicured lawn beyond the terrace.

He was smoking a cheroot. She'd never seen him smoke before, and it gave him an air of mystery. His shoulders, broad and strong, caught the light as the sun outlined him in a golden halo. Close enough to the window, she leaned on the windowsill and drank in the sight of him. How delicious the man was, his bottom particularly delightful in his buckskin breeches.

As if sensing her presence, his gaze lifted, looking toward her suite of rooms, and their eyes met.

Held.

Her breath hitched.

Did he know which room was hers? Surely he did—this was his childhood home, after all, and he must know it better than anyone.

Christopher stopped at the base of the terrace stairs, leaning casually against the stone balustrade. He watched her, his cheroot balanced between two fingers, exuding a nonchalance that only heightened his appeal.

Matilda took in the gardens at his back, but no one else seemed to be about. A daring thought crossed her mind, wicked and thrilling. If he could see her, perhaps she should show him precisely what he was missing.

A smile curved her lips as she considered it.

Determined to make him as uncomfortable as she had been, Matilda stood, water cascading down her bare skin in rivulets that glistened in the sunlight. Meeting Christopher's gaze through the window, she reveled in the shock that flickered across his face, followed by a raw hunger that made her pulse quicken.

For a moment, she let him admire her. Naked, unashamed, and his for the taking—if only he would.

A grin tugged at her lips as she noted the darkening of his expression. His jaw clenched, and his fingers tightened atop the stone terrace as if trying to keep himself grounded.

Before anyone else could stumble upon her display, Matilda stepped out of the bath, wrapped herself in a towel, and moved out of sight.

Her body burned—not with embarrassment, but with anticipation. She ached for him, her earlier release only stoking the fire rather than extinguishing it. Could he truly deny her after what she had just done?

She doubted it.

Dinner tonight would be a battle of restraint, with each glance across the table sparking in the tinderbox of their shared desire.

Matilda smiled as she began to dress, imagining how Christopher's resolve might waver beneath her teasing. Perhaps she would push him further, provoke the lion she so desperately wanted to devour her.

And when she finally had him alone, perhaps he would not be able to resist her.

CHAPTER
EIGHTEEN

Christopher sat at the dinner table that evening, surrounded by family, the local vicar and his wife, the magnificent meal prepared by their ever-reliable cook, which everyone seemed to be enjoying. Yet, despite the perfection of the scene, he was deeply unsatisfied.

Unsatisfied and burning to gain satisfaction from the woman who was seated across from him. She conversed with those around her, her sensual laugh making the hairs on his arms rise and his body harden. And yet, she seemed utterly unaware of his reaction to her. Or simply did not care.

Her mere presence taunted his frayed nerves. He couldn't banish the image of her from earlier —standing in her bedroom window, as naked as the day she was born.

Water had cascaded down her perfect curves, her skin glowing in the sunlight. Her breasts, fully revealed in his memory, made his mouth water. He clenched his jaw, his appetite for food overshadowed by his hunger for her.

Christopher picked up his napkin, laying it across his lap to ensure a semblance of decorum was upheld. He murmured a quick response to Lady Delphine and Lord Lacy, who sat on either side of him before reaching for his wine and taking a long, fortifying sip.

If only he were seated beside Matilda rather than across from her. He wanted—no, needed—to be closer to her, not just tonight but for the rest of their stay at his ancestral home.

When had he fallen so completely under her spell? He wasn't sure, but the realization left him both exhilarated and uneasy.

Lady Delphine cast him another of her longing glances, her delicate features hopeful. He sighed inwardly. She had been doing this all evening, and while he didn't wish to hurt her, he had no interest in encouraging her misplaced affections. He would need to speak to her again —make it clear that the promises they had exchanged as children held no meaning now.

Matilda, meanwhile, seemed determined to torment him. She spoke spiritedly to Charlotte and the local vicar, ignoring his presence. Not once had she glanced his way or even bestowed a little conversation.

Was she ignoring him on purpose? Trying to drive him mad with her indifference?

His mind strayed to their earlier encounter in

his office—a rendezvous that had left them both unsatisfied. He had remained hard for hours after she left, her scent and the memory of her touch haunting him. And then, as if to completely undo him, she had stood naked in her window, a vision of perfection luring him beyond reason.

Had it not been for sheer willpower, he might have stormed upstairs, broken down her door, pulled her from her bath, and carried her to her bed to finish what they had started.

Thrust his hard cock into her wet, willing core and fucked her until they were spent and breathless.

Christopher took a calming breath. With her sitting across from him, he was desperate to shake her calm, collected demeanor. She sat there, every hair in place, her expression serene, as if nothing had happened between them. He wanted to make her lose control, to make her yearn for him as much as he was aching for her.

"I'm so looking forward to visiting the grotto tomorrow, Lord Charteris," Lady Delphine said, with anticipation. "I'm ever so grateful you're willing to take me. It's been years since I last saw it. I think we may have all been children then."

Christopher inwardly winced, having forgotten about the planned excursion. It was another of his parents' schemes to force him and Lady Delphine to spend time together.

"It is no trouble." He raised his voice so the rest of the table could hear. "In fact, if anyone else would like to visit the grotto, you are more than welcome to join us. We'll leave at ten tomorrow morning and have a luncheon in the woods and river. There's a small clearing perfect for a picnic."

"That would be lovely, brother." Charlotte smiled at her husband and then Matilda. "We shall certainly join you."

Matilda's gaze finally met his, and the impact was immediate. Her calm demeanor betrayed nothing, but her eyes—oh, her eyes—sparked with mischief and understanding.

Christopher swallowed.

Hard.

He tamped down the fire she stoked within him. He wished they could escape to the grotto alone, where they could abandon propriety and give in to the wild desire simmering between them.

Let him make her scream his name where no one would hear. Relish the feel of her convulsing about his hard cock, or over his tongue when he made another meal of her.

"That does sound like a wonderful way to spend the day." Matilda's lips curved into an innocent smile that belied the wicked heat in her gaze.

He shifted in his seat, her words stirring images that had no place in a dining room. She was tormenting him, of that he had no doubt.

"So many joining us now. How delightful the day will be," Lady Delphine stated dryly, her words laden with sarcasm.

Christopher ignored her irritation. He had invited others for a reason—being alone with her would only lead to further misunderstandings. Perhaps he would use tomorrow's outing as an opportunity to finally set things straight with her, to explain that he no longer harbored the feelings he once had. That there would be no understanding, nor one forthcoming.

She would be hurt, of course, but better than allowing her to hope for something that would never come to pass.

"I'll have the cook prepare a variety of dishes for your picnic," his mother interjected. "Several servants can meet you there and have everything set up for you all. It will be a splendid outing for the younger members of the house party."

"It will indeed," Lady Delphine agreed, replacing her earlier ire with a smile for his parents.

"Is there not a river near the grotto? Or am I misremembering?" Matilda asked.

"There is," Christopher replied. "And a small boathouse with a wooden rowing boat. It's there year round."

Lady Delphine jumped beside him and clutched at his arm. "Will you take me rowing, my lord? I've never been, and it will be so much fun," Lady Delphine asked, her enthusiasm evident for everyone to see.

Christopher shook his head apologetically. "From what I recall, you cannot swim, Lady Delphine. I wouldn't want to risk your safety."

"That is true," Charlotte interjected. "Falling

into the water while wearing such heavy gowns could be most dangerous."

"But I can swim." Matilda's calm voice floated across to him. "I would love to go rowing with you, Lord Charteris. It sounds most...invigorating."

Christopher's hand clenched around his wine glass. The minx knew what she was doing. The sly smile tugging at her lips was proof enough.

Her words, innocent to the others, carried a far deeper meaning for him. Did she truly want to go rowing? Or did she have other "stimulating" activities in mind?

Images of her sprawled in the boat, her skirts hitched up, her lips parted in pleasure, assaulted his mind. He swallowed hard, forcing the thoughts away.

He clamped his jaw shut, refusing to let her get the better of him. But tomorrow, he vowed, she would not escape unscathed.

He had never brought a woman to climax on a boat before, but there was a first time for everything. Tomorrow would undoubtedly prove both a challenge and an adventure.

CHAPTER
NINETEEN

Matilda kept her distance from Christopher after dinner, deciding to retire early, if only to prove a point that she was worth waiting for and to ignite his longing with the absence of her presence.

Yet the feral, almost uncontrolled emotions she had glimpsed on his face whenever he was waylaid as he tried to approach her left her breathless and unsure of what she had awakened in such a strong, virile man.

Were his emotions growing stronger? Could she hope that mayhap he was falling in love with her, not just lust? Lust, she knew he was already experiencing, but she wanted so much more.

By the following morning, she was dressed in her green morning gown with delicate yellow embroidery, her hair tied low on her nape in a green ribbon, and ready for the informal excursion Christopher was to escort them on to the grotto. The idea of a picnic under the trees and near the river was an inviting prospect, a lovely way to spend a leisurely day away from the estate.

Her maid helped her pin a wide-brimmed straw hat to her natural hair, allowing her to remain cool now that the storm had passed and the day had dawned warm. She doubted anyone would wear a wig today, and if they did, they would soon regret it.

Matilda admired her reflection in the mirror. The natural look lent her an air of sophistication she sometimes lacked. There was always the possibility that one's appearance in society could be too made up.

"The carriages are outside and ready whenever you are, Lady Matilda." Her maid bustled about the room, cleaning up after their morning routine.

"Thank you, Margaret. I'll head down now. When I return, I'd like a bath drawn before dinner."

Margaret curtsied. "Of course, my lady."

Matilda had barely taken several steps along the corridor when a deep, familiar voice murmured near her ear, sending a shiver racing down her spine.

"How am I supposed to keep my hands to myself today, knowing what lies beneath all that pretty material and lace?"

Her stomach fluttered with delicious anticipation. She halted her steps, forcing Christopher to run into her back, his strong hands instinctively gripping her waist to steady them both.

His body pressed against hers, hard and unyielding. His closeness highly improper, yet intoxicating.

"And what makes you think I want you to keep your hands to yourself?" Matilda placed her hand over his, keeping him where he was. "I quite enjoy your touch."

"Your disappearance last evening, your ability to retire without one second in my presence would state otherwise."

She turned to meet his eyes, losing herself in the storm of desire swirling within them. Her lips curved into a teasing smile. "Did you miss me, my lord?" She chuckled. "Are you not more eager this morning to have me to yourself?"

A low, guttural sound escaped him, a mix of frustration and need. It resonated through her, pooling heat low in her belly.

"You shouldn't say such things, for I might drag you into the linen closet and show you how eager I am to be alone with you. I can still see you still on my desk, and the imaginings are pushing me to my limits, Lady Matilda."

She moaned, her fingers brushing along his chiseled jaw. "Do not tease me so, my lord. You do not see me disapproving of your notion to sneak away, and there lies madness."

A muscle ticked in his jaw, and he stepped toward the linen closet he'd just mentioned, his hand lingering at her waist. But before he could act, Charlotte's voice echoed down the hallway.

"Matilda, Christopher! There you are. Come quickly, or we'll be late. Everyone is already waiting outside."

Matilda jumped and schooled her features, hiding her disappointment. She stepped toward the staircase just as Charlotte and Lord Lacy joined them at the top of the stairs.

"Who else besides Lady Delphine is joining us?" Matilda asked Charlotte, keen to speak of everyday things rather than dwell on what she had been about to enjoy with Christopher.

Christopher followed close behind, his presence tangible, even when he wasn't touching her. Occasionally, his hand brushed the small of her back, subtle but deliberate, sending sparks skittering across her skin.

"The vicar and his wife are joining us," Charlotte replied, adjusting her shawl. "Mama suggested they come along after you retired last evening. Lady Delphine is already in your carriage, brother. So you'll travel with us, Matilda."

Disappointment surged through Matilda, knowing she could not be alone with Christopher before the picnic. She fought to look indifferent to the information, but by the time they reached the sunny foyer, she was finding it hard to keep it in place.

As stated, Lady Delphine sat in Christopher's carriage, perched like a peacock with a satisfied smile on her lips. Matilda stifled the urge to yank her off the curricle seat and toss her onto the gravel drive, far away from Christopher.

"I'm happy you'll ride with us, Matilda." Charlotte linked their arms and moved to leave. "I feel like I have not seen you for days."

Matilda nodded, and soon, everyone was seated in their respective vehicles, and the small convoy began its journey down the estate drive toward the grotto.

The day was perfect—warm and cloudless, with the scent of blooming roses and freshly cut grass wafting through the air.

"How has your stay been, my dear? I feel like there is much to catch up on. I hope you're enjoying your time here with us. Oh, how I will miss you when you leave." Charlotte reached for Matilda's hand and gave it a gentle squeeze.

"I've enjoyed myself immensely," Matilda replied. "I'll be quite sad to leave. But at least we'll see Genevieve again, and I'm very much looking forward to that."

Charlotte smiled warmly. "Yes, it has been weeks—far too long." She studied Matilda for a moment, her expression turning curious. "Now that we're alone, I must ask. What's happening between you and my brother?"

Matilda's heart skipped a beat at the forward question. She struggled to formulate a response, and for several heartbeats, her mouth refused to form words. "N-Nothing is happening between us," she replied carefully, not wanting to give herself away. Not yet at least. She wasn't ready to say anything to her friends over what was happening between her and Lord Charteris. "We're friends like you and I are, nothing more."

Lord Lacy chuckled, covering his amusement with a cough as he turned to look out the carriage window.

Charlotte arched an eyebrow at her husband before turning back to Matilda. "I saw you in the hallway this morning. Even though I decided to ignore what I had seen until now, my brother's hands had been on your waist, and you clearly had been standing entirely too close. It looked very intimate. So, I'll ask you again—what is happening between you two?"

Meeting Charlotte's perceptive gaze, Matilda realized there was no point in lying, and Charlotte was her closest friend. She could not lie to her any more than she could lie to herself. "I don't know what is happening," she admitted. "But I know that I like him very much. Perhaps too much that is safe for my heart."

Charlotte's expression softened.

"But he's so determined to remain a bachelor," Matilda continued, her frustration spilling over. "How old does he plan to be before he takes a wife? And then there's Lady Delphine—clearly in love with him and wanting him for herself. I cannot stand it. Do you think he's torn between us? Do you think I am pining for a man who loves another, who only enjoys the game of chasing women but will never truly want one?"

Charlotte shook her head firmly. "No. My

brother is a gentleman. He would never lead a lady along if he did not have genuine feelings for her. His attention to Lady Delphine is merely out of kindness and an old family friendship." She paused. "Perhaps Lady Delphine has been waiting years for something that will never come to pass, and if that is the case, then I am very sorry for her."

"Do you truly think so?" Matilda hoped that was the case, but still, unease warred with her hope.

Charlotte met her eyes, hers shining with conviction. "But the way he looks at you, Matilda—the way he acts around you—it's clear to me that he cares for you very much. Mayhap even more than that."

Matilda's chest tightened with a mixture of longing and doubt. "Do you truly think I have a chance with him?"

The desperation in her question revealed her distress, but she couldn't bring herself to care. Christopher, as her husband, would grant her the freedom she craved and the partnership she longed for. He wouldn't try to change her, to mold her into the perfect duchess. Was he the man she had been searching for?

But how could she make him see her as more than a fleeting tryst? How could she make him fall in love with her and offer her his heart and name?

Charlotte smiled reassuringly. "I believe you do. And I believe he will soon realize it, too.

When one falls for another, it's a gradual surrender—reshaping one's world. I should know. I married the man I love, and I have no doubt you will, too. That man is my brother, Matilda. Just wait and see."

Matilda nodded, clinging to her friend's words with everything she had. Her future happiness depended on it.

CHAPTER
TWENTY

Christopher tried to ignore Lady Delphine, who clung to him whenever the curricle rolled over a small rock or divot in the road. She gasped theatrically, pretending to be far more alarmed than the situation warranted.

Of course, the carriage's elevated height and the uneven country roads could make for a bumpy ride, but she was perfectly safe. He was an accomplished driver and knew these roads better than he knew himself. There was no danger, yet she clutched his arm as if it were the only thing tethering her to this beautiful green earth.

He attempted to free his arm to better control the reins, but she tightened her hold, determined to remain attached to him. Giving up, he sighed inwardly and focused on the distant grotto, yearning for the moment they would arrive so he could finally escape her annoying clutches.

"It is so nice to be alone, is it not?" Lady Delphine tilted up her face with a smile. Her voice carried a syrupy sweetness that made his stomach knot with dread. "We've had so little time together since your return, and I'm quite put out by it."

Christopher's jaw tightened, biting back the words that he was far from concerned about her absence in his life. A telling response from a man toward a woman, and one she ought to heed if she wished for a love match.

"Have you thought any more about our understanding? I thought you might have decided when to inform our parents of our longstanding engagement. I do wish to marry you, as you know."

Dread settled more heavily in his chest. He stared ahead, tightening his grip on the reins as he fought to clear his mind. He didn't want to hurt Lady Delphine—they'd known each other since childhood—but this foolishness needed to end.

"Lady Delphine," he began, his tone measured. "The promise was made when we were children. I do not feel the way I once convinced myself I did. I think it would be best if we both forget that youthful agreement and seek our happiness elsewhere."

He glanced at her, forcing a placating smile, but the glistening tears pooling in her eyes made it clear this would not be the easy conversation he had hoped for.

"I've waited years for you to announce our

engagement." She swiped at a lone tear, her hand trembling. "I've been patient, Christopher. I did not push you or write letters demanding that you honor your promise, and now you're saying you've changed your mind? That we were too young to understand what we wanted? I refuse to believe you would treat me so poorly, especially when at the lake you made me believe we would be announcing our happy news soon."

He sighed, keeping his gaze on the road ahead. "Delphine, I do not want to argue with you, but we were children. I barely knew what I was asking of you. I hoped, in time, that you would find love elsewhere, as I was not seeking marriage myself. But I cannot let you continue to believe there is a future between us. It was wrong of me to give you hope at the lake that day, but I did not wish to ruin your visit here in Kent. But I do not wish to marry you. I am very sorry."

Her lower lip trembled, and she blinked quickly. "I'm seven and twenty, Christopher. No one will want to marry me now. I'm practically an old maid."

"That is not true," he rebuked. "You're beautiful, Delphine, and an heiress. Countless men would court you if you were to attend the London Season and consort with your peers. But I am not the one for you and never will be. I cannot give you the happiness you deserve."

She shook her head stubbornly. "I think you should let me be the judge of that."

He drew in a steadying breath, knowing he needed to be direct, no matter how much it might sting. "I do not love you, Delphine. I'm sorry to speak so plainly, but it's the truth. This arrangement—this mistake of our making—should have been set aside long ago. I cannot offer you what you want, and I won't pretend otherwise."

She moved away from him, silent now, and he felt a pang of guilt for his harshness.

"I suppose Lady Matilda is the reason you've changed your mind," she countered with accusation.

Christopher almost choked on the denial that rushed to his lips. "Of course not," he quickly countered. "This has nothing to do with Lady Matilda or anyone else. My feelings—or lack thereof—are independent of anyone else. Please understand that."

Her lips pressed into a thin line. "Whatever you say, Lord Charteris. I'm sure, in time, I'll find a match better suited to my character than you ever could have been."

He ignored the barb and tried to ease the tension. "You will see. When you meet a man who truly adores you, you'll understand why I've said what I have today. I do not say this to hurt you but to ensure your future is happier than I could make it."

He pulled the carriage to a stop near the picnic location, setting the brake before climbing down to assist her. She stepped off the carriage with practiced grace, avoiding his gaze as she adjusted her skirts.

The other carriages soon arrived, and under the shade of a copse of trees, the servants began setting up a picturesque picnic with blankets, cushions, and baskets of food.

"Oh, it's been far too long since I was last here." All but bouncing with excitement, Charlotte tugged her husband toward the lake that glittered in the sunlight.

"This way to the grotto," Christopher called, motioning for the remaining guests to follow. Yet, glancing over his shoulder, he saw that only one person had heeded his invitation.

Matilda.

He paused, watching her approach with a lightness in her step that belied the teasing glint in her eyes.

"Where is everyone else?" he asked, feigning confusion. "I thought we were here to see the grotto, not the lake."

Matilda glanced back at the others. Charlotte, the reverend, and his wife had all drifted toward the water while Lady Delphine seated herself on a picnic blanket and sipped lemonade.

"I suppose they had other priorities." Matilda shrugged. "But I want to see the grotto—if you're still willing to show me."

He smiled despite himself. "I'd be willing to show you anything," he blurted before realizing the implication of his words.

Matilda's lips twitched. "Really?" Her tone

playful. "After yesterday's disappointing lesson in your office, I'm not sure you should make promises of pleasurable outings unless you intend to follow through."

His body tensed, desire flaring to life as he led her into the grotto. Once they were out of sight of the others, he couldn't hold back any longer.

Christopher slipped his arm around her waist and pulled her into a shadowy corner. "You think I didn't suffer yesterday, not being able to finish you off as I wanted?" he growled, his breath hot against her ear. "I was hard for hours, Matilda. I hungered for your taste, to hear your breathless cries of my name that never came. And then, last evening, just when I was free from our guests, you slipped off to bed before I could steal you away."

Her arms looped around his neck, her smile a Siren call. "Well," she murmured, her voice flowing over him like silk, "I'm here now."

He didn't hesitate. Lowering his head, he captured her lips in a kiss that spoke of all the frustration, longing, and passion that had consumed him since their last encounter. But even as the kiss deepened, he knew one thing for certain.

It would never be enough.

CHAPTER
TWENTY-ONE

The cool stone made Matilda gasp as Christopher pressed her against the rough wall, his lips capturing hers with a hunger that made her pulse race. His kiss was fierce, demanding, like a man starved of air, and she responded with equal fervor. She had been desperate for him since leaving his office yesterday, and now, the intensity of his need ignited her own, leaving her trembling with anticipation.

The damp chill of the grotto wrapped around them, mingling with the heat radiating from their entwined bodies. Her back arched instinctively, pressing her curves against his hard frame. She clutched at the rich fabric of his coat, using him for balance as her knees threatened to buckle.

His lips left hers to trail a line of kisses down her neck, the scrape of his stubble a delicious contrast to the softness of his mouth. She tilted her head back, exposing more of her throat to his ministrations, as the muted trickle of water somewhere in the grotto provided a faint, rhythmic melody to their stolen moment.

"I cannot help myself," Christopher murmured. "I must feel you."

Matilda nodded, her breath coming in short, desperate gasps. Words failed her as his hands moved to the hem of her gown, bunching the fabric and exposing her legs to the cool cave air. The sensation made her shiver, not from the chill, but the anticipation thrumming through her veins.

Her fingers threaded into his hair, holding him close as he worked to push aside the layers of undergarments and skirts in his way. His warm hand finally found her bare skin, and she exhaled a shaky breath when his fingers grazed the sensitive flesh between her thighs.

"You're so wet, Matilda." His lips brushed her ear as his hand moved higher. "You're a naughty little minx."

She moaned as he stroked her, his touch unhurried but maddeningly thorough. Heat pooled at her core as his fingers found the sweet spot that made her tremble. Needing him closer, she hooked one leg over his hip, granting him better access.

His eyes widened at her boldness, and a wicked smile curved his lips. "I cannot get enough of you," he growled. His fingers pressed deeper, teasing and stroking with practiced skill.

Matilda clung to his shoulders, her breaths mingling with his as pleasure coursed through her. "More," she gasped, closing her eyes to revel in his touch. "I need you, Christopher."

He groaned in response, his free hand gripping her waist as his fingers plunged into her slick heat, his movements echoing the rhythm of their shared desire.

Her climax came swiftly, taking her by surprise as waves of pleasure crashed over her. She cried out his name, the keen echoing off the stone walls, and he captured her moans with a bruising kiss. His tongue swept into her mouth, tangling with hers as he swallowed every mutter she made.

He withdrew his clever fingers and adjusted her skirts only when her trembling had subsided. His dark eyes watched her intently, a flicker of fever in their depths. The air between them crackled with unfinished need, and Matilda's pulse quickened.

"Tell me what I can do for you." Her hand located the bulge straining against the front of his breeches. Her fingers wrapped around his large, long manhood, stroking. "You must be so desirous. Let me make you feel as good as you just made me."

His hand covered hers, guiding her movements for a moment before he stepped back and shook his head. "Not here. But tonight. Come to my room at midnight, and I'll teach you what you can do for me."

Her cheeks flushed at his words, but she met his gaze boldly. "I've read a great deal, you know. Do you mean to have me take you into my mouth?"

His eyes widened in surprise before a deep chuckle rumbled from his chest. The sound was low and seductive, making her stomach flutter. "You surprise me, Matilda." A wicked grin played on his lips. "Is there anything that would shock you?"

"No." She lifted her chin and smiled, though her heart raced at the prospect of what they had planned. She had never been so intimate with a man, and no matter how much she wanted Christopher, this desire and lust were all new to her. A different stage in her otherwise sheltered life.

What if she disappointed him? What if she was not enough?

She stepped closer, her hands moving to the buttons of his breeches. He caught her wrists, his grip firm but not harsh. "Not here," he insisted again, though his resolve was weakening.

"Just a little taste," she pleaded, pleased to sound unperturbed and coaxing, the opposite of the worries tumbling about her mind. But if she started her journey here and now, she would not be so nervous when she went to his room at midnight.

"If we hear anyone coming, I'll stop. Please, Christopher. I want to do this for you."

His growl of frustration, along with the softening of his grip on her wrists, was all the answer she needed. She undid the fastenings of his breeches with deft fingers, freeing him. Her breath hitched at the sight of his member, a heady mix of nervousness and excitement thrumming through her blood.

"Matilda," he groaned, his head falling back as her tongue flicked over the tip of his length. "Christ, don't tease me. We don't have much time."

She smiled before taking him into her mouth, her movements tentative at first but growing bolder as his moans encouraged her. Her hand wrapped around the base of him, stroking his thickness in time with her mouth as she worked him.

His fingers tangled in her hair, guiding her firmly. The sounds he made, raw and unrestrained, spurred her on to take him deeper.

"Matilda," he rasped. "Goddamn it, I cannot come in your mouth."

She released him with a pop, her hand continuing its rhythm as she met his gaze. "You can," she said, pressing her legs together as the sweet ache teased her once more. "I want you to. I want to taste you, Christopher."

He swore under his breath, his hands tightening on her shoulders as if to steady himself. "You're going to ruin me," he muttered before she took him into her mouth and halted his exchange.

This time, there was no hesitation. She

worked him with single-minded focus, her tongue swirling around his chiseled cock, before sucking him hard. She felt him tremble, knew he was leaning on the wall at her back for support. His hips bucked, his control slipping as he neared his release.

"Your mouth is wicked," he growled. "Suck me harder, my darling."

With a shuddering groan, he spilled into her mouth, and she swallowed every ounce of his pleasure, savoring the taste of him. She did not stop until he was spent and flaccid in her hand.

He wrenched her to her feet and kissed her fiercely. His lips crushed hers as his hands framed her face. The taste of himself on her tongue seemed to ignite something primal within him, and he deepened the kiss, leaving them breathless.

"Midnight," he ordered, brooking no argument. "Do not be late, or I'll come looking for you."

Matilda nodded, pleased that she had been brave enough to give him pleasure, too. They stepped apart and adjusted their clothing before leaving the grotto.

When they returned, the picnic was in full swing, and the air was filled with laughter and clinking crystal glasses. Matilda made her way to Charlotte, accepting a glass of champagne and sinking onto a blanket beside her friend.

Sitting across from her, Christopher leaned on one hand as he reached for a strawberry. His eyes never left hers as he bit into the fruit, licking the juice from his fingers in a way that made her cheeks flush. She could still feel those fingers inside her, bringing her to exquisite heights, and the memory sent a fresh wave of heat through her.

She sipped her champagne, trying to appear unaffected, but the hunger in Christopher's gaze mirrored hers.

How was she ever to leave here? Leave him? He was everything she had ever wanted, and no one else could compare.

Her resolve hardened as she watched him. She would win his heart, whatever it took. He was hers—he just didn't know it yet.

And by the end of her stay at his family estate, she intended to make sure he did.

CHAPTER
TWENTY-TWO

Matilda settled with others on the picnic blankets, the sunlight dappling through the trees, casting fleeting patterns across their gathering. She tried to ignore the satisfaction that still hummed through her veins after being alone with Christopher. The memory of his touch, his lips, and the desperate passion they shared in the grotto made her heart race and her skin flush with warmth.

In all her years attending the Season, mingling with suitors, and enduring the half-hearted attentions of gentlemen admirers, she had never felt such an overwhelming sense of rightness as when she was with Christopher. Everything fell into place with him—her desires, her dreams, her very sense of self.

She sipped her champagne, its cool bubbling doing little to ease the heat rising within her. The lively conversation around her barely registered.

He consumed her thoughts, and inevitably, her gaze sought him out again and again.

Christopher continued to lean against a pile of plush cushions. Just as their eyes met, he popped another ripe strawberry into his mouth. Her stomach clenched with longing, a fresh wave of hunger overtaking her. How was it possible to still want him after what had transpired mere minutes ago?

She clenched her hands in her lap, struggling to maintain her composure. How was she to keep herself from throwing caution—and propriety—to the wind and throwing herself at him right here, in front of everyone?

"What a beautiful spot, Lord Charteris." Lady Delphine's voice was exceedingly sweet as she shifted closer to Christopher. "I cannot thank you enough for bringing me here."

Matilda's smile froze. Lady Delphine's intention was clear to anyone with eyes. The woman's movements were deliberate, her manner saccharine. It was unmistakable she wanted Christopher as her husband and seemed determined to secure her prize.

Matilda's heart tightened. There may have been a time when she would have let Lady Delphine have her way without a second thought, but not now. Not when her feelings for Christopher had grown into something undeniable, something she could not ignore.

Surely, their connection, the fiery chemistry that burned whenever they were near each other, was mutual. She couldn't have imagined the desire in his dark eyes or the passion in his touch.

Lady Delphine's syrupy smile widened. "I must say, it's a joy to have everyone together. In fact..." She paused dramatically, her gaze flicking to Christopher, who looked up with a faint frown. "I believe this is the perfect moment to share some wonderful news."

Matilda stilled, her heart thudding loudly in her chest. Whatever news was she talking of? She had not heard of anything untoward or newsworthy that had happened at the ducal estate.

Lady Delphine's voice turned coy, her smile triumphant. "Lord Charteris and I have an announcement to make."

Christopher sat up, his frown deepening. "We do?" He cleared his throat and moved to close the space to Lady Delphine. "I do not believe there is anything to say..."

Lady Delphine's laugh was high-pitched and brittle and broke into Christophers words. "Don't be coy, my darling lord. This is no time for teasing."

Darling...

Matilda met Christopher's eyes and saw the apprehension in his brown gaze.

Lady Delphine turned to the gathered guests, her eyes sparkling with excitement. "Since we were young adults—we have been secretly engaged! But now, there is no longer a need to keep it a secret." She paused, smiling at everyone in their party. "Do you not wish us happy?"

The words struck Matilda like a physical blow. Her ears rang, and her grip on her champagne glass tightened.

"Lord Charteris asked me for my hand in marriage over ten years ago, and I joyfully accepted." Lady Delphine clapped her hands as if she had just declared the most delightful news in the world. "Now that we are of an age where delaying is no longer wise, I thought it was time to announce our impending union."

Matilda watched Christopher, who appeared utterly bewildered. His lips parted as if to speak, but no words came.

"Lady Delphine," he began, glaring at her in warning. "What are you doing?"

Lady Delphine's laugh tinkled like a bell, but it resembled a death knell to Matilda. "I informed our parents this morning, and they are, of course, overjoyed. We shall be married within the month, and you are invited." She turned to them all, her eyes bright with triumph. "Isn't it wonderful? Even you shall attend, Lady Matilda, before you depart the estate."

The world seemed to tilt, and the cheerful chatter of the other guests turned into an indistinct hum, blending with the pounding of her heart. Charlotte congratulated her brother and Lady Delphine, and the vicar offered his services for the ceremony.

All were so happy for the couple, but Matilda could not breathe.

Her thoughts tumbled in a chaotic whirl of

disbelief and betrayal. Engaged? To Lady Delphine? After everything they had shared—after everything he had whispered to her—how could this be happening?

Her gaze found Christopher's, searching for answers, but his expression was unreadable. He looked as though he had been blindsided, yet he said nothing to refute Lady Delphine's claims. He did not try to salvage a future between herself and his lordship.

"You've been secretly engaged?" Matilda's voice broke through the fog of conversation, trembling with barely restrained anger. "Is that why you've insisted you have no interest in marriage? Because you were never truly free to choose?"

Lady Delphine turned to her, her expression one of feigned innocence. "Oh, dear Lady Matilda, I understand why you might be surprised. But yes, we've been betrothed for years. It was our little secret, wasn't it, Christopher?" She beamed at him, though her grip on his arm tightened possessively.

Christopher opened his mouth as if to speak, but Lady Delphine forged ahead. "It was difficult, of course, to keep our love concealed. But we thought it best until the time was right. And now, the wait is over. I can finally celebrate our union openly and begin planning the wedding we've both dreamed of."

The sharp ache in Matilda's chest was unbearable. She couldn't reconcile the man who had kissed her, touched her, and whispered promises in the grotto with the one sitting silently beside Lady Delphine.

Her cheeks burned with humiliation, and she swallowed the lump in her throat. She had been a fool. He had used her, and she had let him like some stupid harlequin she was not.

"Well..." Her voice sounded brittle, even to her ears. "Congratulations to you both. I'm sure everyone will be eager to begin planning your nuptials."

Standing abruptly, she placed her glass on the blanket and turned toward the carriages.

"Lady Matilda," Christopher called after her with an urgency she'd not heard before. She ignored him, quickening her pace as tears pricked her eyes.

He caught up with her just as she reached the carriages, his hand closing around her arm. "Matilda, please wait."

She wrenched her arm free, her eyes flashing with anger. "What could you possibly have to say to me, my lord? Commiserations? An apology? Spare me your excuses. I have no interest in hearing them."

"Let me explain," he pleaded, a desperate edge to his words. "This isn't what I want. I swear to you—"

"Swear to me?" she yelled, interrupting him. "Swear to me when everything you've said and done has been a lie? You let me believe..." Her voice broke, and she drew in a shuddering breath. "You let me believe I mattered to you. That we..."

Her words faltered, and she shook her head. "I was a fool to trust you. But no longer. I'm leaving."

"Don't." He reached for her hand. "Please do not leave like this."

She wrenched away. "I'm going to Genevieve's. She needs me, and I cannot stay here another moment."

"Matilda," he implored.

Her eyes locked with his, and for a fleeting moment, she saw the regret in his gaze. But it wasn't enough. It would never be enough.

"Goodbye, Christopher." She stepped into the carriage and closed the door.

Through the window, she saw him move back, his hands clenched at his sides as the carriage rolled away. Lady Delphine's smug expression lingered in her mind, a bitter reminder of the triumph she had claimed at her expense.

Matilda's heart ached, but her resolve hardened. She would leave this place, leave him, and never look back.

But as the carriage rumbled away, she couldn't stop the silent tears that slipped down her cheeks.

He was the one man she had ever truly wanted; now, he was lost to her.

Forever.

CHAPTER
TWENTY-THREE

Lady Delphine trailed after Christopher, her footsteps deliberate as she approached the line of carriages. Christopher paced the area, his eyes fixed on the retreating carriage carrying Matilda away. As it disappeared from view, a wave of panic surged through him.

Had he lost her for good?

He ran a hand through his hair in frustration, his thoughts racing. The weight of Lady Delphine's earlier announcement bore down on him like a leaden shroud, and with sinking certainty, he realized he had.

"Lady Delphine, what are you thinking about announcing our faux engagement like that?" He clasped her hand and marched her toward an enclosed carriage, needing to return home posthaste and clear this horrible mess Lady Delphine had created.

"We, madam, are not engaged, " he growled,

barely containing his anger. His stomach churned, a storm of emotions roiling inside him as he tried to fathom how to fix the disaster Lady Delphine had so brazenly created.

Lady Delphine settled into the plush squabs with infuriating calm, her gloved hands smoothing her skirts. "You asked for my hand." She remained composed, though her eyes glinted with calculation. "I am simply holding you to your word. Our parents are delighted, and I am, too. I've never stopped loving you, Christopher, and I am ready to become your wife. You should not have made your proposal if you did not mean it."

Christopher slammed the carriage door shut, the sound echoing like a gunshot in the enclosed space. He dropped onto the seat opposite her, his jaw tight with frustration. "What is wrong with you, Delphine? Do you truly believe this is acceptable? We were children. Children! That promise meant nothing then, and it certainly does not mean anything now."

Her lips curved into a practiced pout that might have seemed innocent without the stone beneath it. "I am seven and twenty, my lord. At my age, few men will offer marriage. I have not had a Season nor sought suitors because I trusted your word. You asked me to be your wife, and I waited patiently for you. Perhaps you should apologize for your lapse in judgment rather than chastise me for expecting you to honor it."

He dragged a hand through his hair, fighting

the urge to bellow. "I will not marry you. As soon as we return to the estate, I will amend this catastrophic error and see that you understand the truth of the matter. Then you will leave my home and return to yours."

Lady Delphine's smile tightened, but her composure did not falter. "If you wish to create a scandal, by all means, dissolve the engagement. But I assure you, the whispers will follow you—and Lady Matilda. Everyone saw her flee the picnic in tears after our secret engagement was announced. Do you think society will not put the piece together and assume the worst of her?"

Her words struck like a blow, and he recoiled, his breath catching. "I do not wish to hurt Matilda."

"Then I suggest you do not." Delphine's tone was smooth as silk. "Do the honorable thing, Christopher. Marry me, as you promised. Lady Matilda will find someone else, someone more suited to her. As for you, I will be a devoted wife and ensure our union is one to be envied."

Her words twisted like a knife in his chest. Devoted wife? She might as well have said jailer.

The carriage rolled to a stop after what felt like eons stuck in the carriage with Lady Delphine. Christopher seized the moment, leaping down before the footman could open the door. He strode into the house, his pulse thundering as he scanned the foyer.

Relief poured through him but for a moment at the sight of her—Matilda.

Luggage cases surrounded her. She spoke in hushed tones with his parents and sister, her words steady though her eyes betrayed the storm within her.

"Lady Matilda," Christopher called, his heart clenching as she turned to face him.

Her pleasant smile was a facade, her expression too composed, too polite. She dipped into a curtsy. "Lord Charteris."

"You're leaving?" His words came out more a statement than a question.

"Yes," she replied, as cooly as the marble beneath their feet. "I think it's time I begin my journey to Lady Genevieve's. She'll be having her baby soon, and I wish to be there for her. Charlotte will join us in a week or two."

"Have a safe journey, Lady Matilda," Delphine interjected, appearing at his side and slipping her arm through his as if she belonged there. The gesture sent a fresh wave of guilt and rage crashing over him.

"Congratulations again to you both." Matilda's voice was steady, but her eyes gleamed with unshed tears. "I'm certain you'll be very happy together."

Delphine's lips curled into a triumphant smile. "I'm certain we shall." She paused, her gaze as sharp as a blade. "Will you attend our wedding, Lady Matilda? We would so like to have our friends there to celebrate."

Matilda leaned down to pick up a small valise, her movements slow and deliberate. "I'm afraid I cannot. The Tyndall estate is a considerable distance from here, and I won't be able to make such a journey so soon after leaving. But I will be thinking of you both."

A footman entered the foyer and bowed. "Lady Matilda, your carriage is ready. Shall we collect your cases now, my lady?"

"Yes, thank you." She started toward the door, Christopher's chest tightening as he watched her turn away. Every fiber of his being screamed at him to stop her.

"Excuse me," he muttered, untangling himself from Delphine's grip and following Matilda outside.

He caught up with her just as she was about to enter the carriage. "Matilda, you cannot leave. Do not leave. Let me attempt to rectify this farce."

She froze, one foot on the step, before turning to face him. "Fix what?" she asked, her response laced with disbelief. "How can you fix anything, Christopher? You've been secretly engaged to Lady Delphine for years. Whether it was a mistake of youth or not, you owe her your hand."

She stepped into the carriage and sank onto the squabs, her movements graceful even as her composure began to unravel. Her blue eyes, glistening with restrained emotion, met his. "You should be commended for doing the honorable thing. Lady Delphine adores you—it's clear to everyone—and she will make a good wife. She will try her best to make you happy. There are worse fates."

"Worse fates?" He could not think of any right at this moment. "Matilda, there is no fate worse than the one I now find myself in. Do not leave me. Please."

She gave a soft, humorless laugh, leaning forward to speak through the open window. "But that's where you're wrong, my lord. My fate is worse. I will live my life loving a man who married another. The result is the same whether it was out of obligation, duty, or love. You will marry her, and I will become the spinster. A wealthy one, perhaps, but a spinster nonetheless. I would have preferred a life here with you." The vulnerability in her words cut through him like a blade. "I think we could have been happy, Christopher. I know I would have been."

He reached for her hand, gripping her tightly. "I'll resolve this, Matilda. I promise."

She pulled her hand free, her expression hardening. "Don't make promises you cannot keep. Your path is set, and so is mine." She leaned back, distant and aloof. "I wish you happiness, Lord Charteris. Be kind to Lady Delphine—she is innocent in all this."

Christopher stepped back as the carriage lurched forward, his hand falling uselessly to his side. He stood frozen a second time in one day, watching the vehicle disappear down the drive, taking Matilda with it.

The emptiness that followed was crushing, a hollow ache that threatened to consume him.

What have I done?

He turned sharply, his jaw tightening with determination. Whatever it took, he would end this farce of an engagement. Delphine's scheming had cost him the woman he loved.

His steps skidded to a stop on the gravel.

Love?

He took a deep breath, knowing deep within his heart that what he felt for Matilda was true. Was love.

He loved her. No, he adored her and would win her back.

He would not let his youthful folly cost him his future.

Without hesitation, he strode back into the house, the weight of his decision settling heavily on his shoulders and the consequences that determination would bring.

No time like the present.

CHAPTER
TWENTY-FOUR

Matilda had not made it far from the D'Estel estate before her driver was forced to pull over at the Crown and Stag Inn, a well-kept but modest establishment perched at the edge of the London to Dover road. Heavy rain had turned the road into a treacherous quagmire, and a flooded causeway several miles ahead had rendered it utterly impassable.

The innkeeper informed her that with such relentless rain, it might be a day or two before the waters receded and the road became passable again. Fortunately, she had arrived ahead of other stranded travelers, securing rooms for herself and her staff before the inn's yard became inundated with carriages, horses, and desperate drivers seeking refuge.

Matilda stood at the window of her small but tidy room, watching the chaos unfold. As grooms scurried to tend the horses, lanterns bobbed through the rain-soaked courtyard. Drivers shouted orders, their voices nearly drowned out by the relentless drumming of rain on the cobblestones.

The faint scent of damp straw and wet earth drifted in through the cracks of the old window frame, mingling with the aroma of wood smoke from a roaring fire her maid, Margaret, had diligently stoked. The warmth of the flames did little to thaw the cold knot of despair that had taken up residence in Matilda's chest.

Christopher.

His name echoed in her mind, conjuring the memory of his anguished expression as she'd left the D'Estel estate. She had wanted to believe his promises, but her heart had told her otherwise. A man bound by honor—and by an engagement, no matter how ill-conceived—could not be hers.

Margaret bustled about the room, laying out her nightclothes and setting fresh wash water on the stand.

"I shall be next door, my lady unless you require anything else for the evening. Your dinner has been ordered and will be brought up shortly."

"Thank you, Margaret. That will be all for now."

Her maid dipped into a curtsy and left, leaving Matilda alone with her thoughts. She turned to the window, her fingers trailing over the cool glass as she gazed at the rain-drenched landscape. For a fleeting moment, she considered returning to the D'Estel estate. But what would be the point? Christopher had made his choices—choices that no amount of protest on his part could change.

She sank into the chair at the small desk, her hand trembling as she reached for pen and paper. She needed advice, and there was only one person she could confide in without fear of judgment.

Dearest Charlotte, she began, her writing slow and deliberate.
I find myself stranded at the Crown and Stag Inn due to the flooded causeway. The innkeeper believes it will take at least two days for the waters to recede, perhaps longer if the storm persists. I write to ask your counsel. Do such storms often damage the causeway? Should I abandon my journey to Genevieve's altogether and return to the estate?

Her pen hovered above the paper as she debated whether to write more. She longed to tell Charlotte everything—the truth about Christopher, her despair at losing him, her shame at being drawn into such a hopeless tangle. But how could she, when Charlotte was so delighted by her brother's engagement to Lady Delphine?

A light knock at the door interrupted her thoughts.

"Your dinner, my lady." A young maid stepped into view with a tray laden with roast beef stew, fresh bread, cheese, and a steaming cup of tea.

"Thank you." Matilda smiled in thanks. "The dinner looks delicious."

The maid curtsied and placed the tray on the table. "If there's anything else you require, please ring the bell, my lady."

"Wait," Matilda said, holding out the folded letter. "Please have this sent to the D'Estel estate posthaste."

The maid's eyes widened at the mention of the duke's estate, but she nodded eagerly. "Of course, my lady. Posthaste."

Alone once more, Matilda sat at the table and slowly ate her meal, savoring the warmth and richness of the stew. The bread was soft and fresh, the cheese sharp and tangy, and the tea soothed her frayed nerves. Yet even the comforting meal could not lift the heavy weight pressing on her heart.

After dinner, she moved to the armchair by the fire, cradling a glass of wine as she stared into the flames. The flickering light cast dancing shadows on the walls and the rhythmic drumming of the rain against the window provided a melancholy accompaniment to her thoughts.

Christopher, she thought again, her chest tightening. How foolish she had been to let herself hope. The memory of his touch, his whispered promises—they had felt so real, so achingly perfect. But reality had come crashing down around her at the picnic, and she could no longer deny the truth.

He was bound to Lady Delphine by honor if not by love.

Tears pricked at her eyes, but she refused to let them fall. She was stronger than this. She had to be.

The following day brought no respite from the storm. Rain lashed against the windows with unrelenting fury, and the wind howled like a mournful specter. Matilda remained confined to her room, the inn's common areas overrun with travelers and coachmen seeking refuge.

Margaret joined her in the late morning, carrying a small, wooden playing card box. "The weather shows no signs of improving, my lady. Shall we pass the time with a game?"

Matilda hesitated, then nodded. "Yes, I suppose that's as good a way as any to occupy the day."

They sat at the small table near the window, the cards spread out before them. The patter of rain and the occasional creak of the inn's timbers were the only sounds as they played hand after hand, their conversation light and inconsequential.

Yet Matilda's thoughts remained far away. Each time she glanced out at the gray, rain-soaked yard, her mind conjured the image of

Christopher standing in the foyer, his expression torn between desperation and regret.

"Are you all right, my lady?" Margaret asked, breaking the silence.

Matilda forced a smile. "I'm fine, Margaret. Just tired."

Her maid nodded, though her eyes were filled with quiet concern.

By the time evening fell, the storm showed no sign of abating. Matilda dined in her room again. The meal was as well prepared as the previous night but offered little comfort. She felt trapped —by the weather, by her circumstances, by her own heart.

As she lay in bed that night, listening to the relentless pounding of rain, she cried for the first time since leaving the D'Estel estate. Silent tears slid down her cheeks, soaking into the pillow as her chest ached with a grief she could not shake.

She had lost him.

She had lost the one man who had ever made her feel truly alive. And no matter how much she wished it were otherwise, there was no escaping the truth.

When sleep finally claimed her, it was fitful and plagued by dreams of Christopher—dreams in which he reached for her, only to be pulled away by the shadowy figure of Lady Delphine.

A true nightmare, even in her wakeful hours.

CHAPTER
TWENTY-FIVE

Christopher sat across from Charlotte the following morning, the warm light of the sun filtering through the breakfast room's lace curtains. The faint clink of silverware provided a comforting backdrop as they shared their morning meal.

"A missive, Lady Lacy."

"Oh, thank you." Charlotte severed the silence as she accepted a note from a servant. She broke the seal and scanned the note, a slight frown settling on her brow before she said, "Oh dear."

"Is something amiss, sister?" Christopher asked, hoping the letter she was reading did not include dreadful news. There was enough melancholy in the house already without adding more.

He sipped his coffee, hoping it would banish the weariness of a sleepless night wrestling with his thoughts. Thoughts on how to break his betrothal. Thoughts on how he could win back Matilda's trust and affection.

Charlotte folded the note and placed it on the table with a sigh. "It's from Lady Matilda. She's stranded at the Crown and Stag Inn due to last night's storm. The road is flooded, and she fears it may remain impassable for some days. She asks if we have any insight into how long such conditions might last."

Christopher frowned and set down his cup. "London to Devon road? It's been known to remain impassable after heavy rain for a week or more. She cannot stay at that inn alone for days. It's unsafe for a woman of her means, and she only has her maid and coachman for safety."

Charlotte's lips pressed into a thin line as she took in his words. "Indeed. She mentions only her maid as company. An inn filled with men of questionable character is no place for a young lady of her standing. What should we do? Shall we advise her to remain there or return here?"

"There is no choice to make," Christopher replied firmly. "I'll take the carriage and fetch her myself. She must return to the D'Estel estate. Leaving her there is out of the question."

Charlotte nodded in agreement. "Yes, you must fetch her, but Christopher..." She hesitated. "Are you certain this is wise? Your engagement—"

"Is my affair to manage," he interrupted, not wanting to be reminded of the fiasco he was in.

"But right now Lady Matilda's safety is paramount."

Charlotte sighed but did not press further. After all, she knew his stubborn streak well.

Christopher stood, his determination rekindled, and rang for the servants to ready the carriage. Within the hour, he was on the road, his carriage wheels churning through the mud-slicked tracks as the countryside sped past.

As the inn came into view several hours later, Christopher's pulse quickened. The sight of the modest, weather-beaten building filled him with unease. He strode into the yard and exchanged a few gold coins for the innkeeper's cooperation before ascending the narrow, creaking staircase to Matilda's room.

There was a brief rustle of movement when he knocked, and then the door opened. Matilda stood before him, her honeyed hair framing her face, her expression a mixture of surprise and something more profound—hope, perhaps?

"Lord Charteris?" she said, breathless. "What are you doing here?"

Christopher stepped inside without waiting for an invitation, taking in the modest but clean space. The scent of lavender lingered in the air, mingling with the aroma of damp wood and smoke from the hearth. He turned toward her, noting the way the faint afternoon light illuminated her features.

"Charlotte received your missive." Hell, she

was pretty and by God he'd missed the sight of her. "I came at once. You cannot stay here, Matilda. It's not safe."

Matilda hesitated, her delicate fingers gripping the edge of the door as though she might retreat. "I have no desire to impose on your family, especially with your—" She faltered. "Your fiancée."

Christopher's jaw tightened. "That engagement is a farce, and I shall deal with it. But you must not stay here. This inn is no place for a duke's daughter. Your safety is my only concern."

"Is it?" she countered, bitterness edging her words. "Do you insist on rescuing me simply to avoid your family being held accountable should anything untoward occur?"

He stared at her, taken aback. "You believe I would be motivated solely by obligation?"

She folded her arms, an action that drew his gaze—however reluctantly—to the rise and fall of her chest. "Why else would you come, my lord?" she asked coolly. "There is no place for me in your life."

"Matilda..." He took a step closer, the intimacy of the small room amplifying the tension between them. Hell, he wanted her. Even now, when she was loathe to see him, he wanted nothing more than to take her in his arms and comfort her.

"I came because I care. Because I could not forgive myself if harm came to you."

She scoffed, slamming the door closed and

giving him her back as she started toward the fire. "Care? Do not mock me."

"I am not mocking you." His tone was earnest as he tried to make her believe him. "I care for you, Matilda. I love you. And I would rather face the scorn of all England than see you spend another moment here, alone and vulnerable."

Her shoulders stiffened, and she turned to face him, her eyes brimming with tears. "You love me?" She shook her head in skepticism. "Yet you allowed yourself to become bound to another."

"Because I am a fool," he admitted, closing the distance between them. "A coward who feared what loving you might cost me. But I cannot deny it any longer. Every moment I am without you feels like a lifetime wasted."

The space between them seemed to shrink until it was almost nonexistent. Matilda's breath hitched as she gazed up at him, and he could see her resolve to hate him was crumbling.

"Christopher..."

"Come with me," he pleaded. "Let me take you home. Let me prove that my love for you is more than words."

She hesitated, her lips parting as though to argue, but whatever protest she might have made dissolved into silence. The air crackled with unspoken longing, the weight of their shared grief and unfulfilled desire pressing upon them like a tangible force.

At last, she nodded. "Very well."

Christopher exhaled, relief flooding him.

"Thank you," he murmured, his hand brushing hers in a touch that lingered a moment too long.

"You should not touch me for I cannot trust myself." Matilda whispered, though her words lacked conviction. She was glad he had come, that he was here, and that she wasn't so alone in the world.

Her body hungered for him, and even now, angry as she was at the situation in which they now found themselves, she knew that the man before her was the one she wished to marry.

The man she loved.

"I had no choice. I could not leave you here alone, not with the storm, not with the risk—" He stopped, raking a hand through his dark hair, his frustration palpable. "Matilda, do you not understand? I couldn't bear the thought of you being in danger. You were alone with only your maid and elderly driver."

She shivered, having not thought of the danger she could be in should anyone untoward find out that she was here, practically alone. "I am perfectly safe," she lied, knowing that she was probably far from being so. "You should return home to your betrothed."

Christopher stepped closer, the space between them shrinking with each determined stride. He was so overbearing, tall, and seemed to suck all the air out of the room where they were standing. "There is no engagement," he said firmly. "There never was. Not in any way that mattered. Please, Matilda, believe me."

His vision blurred, and she swallowed hard, determined not to lose her composure. She tipped up her chin, needing to find the strength to finish this conversation with Christopher. Possibly one of the last she would ever have with him.

"Lady Delphine announced your engagement to everyone. She expects you to honor your word, as does your family. There is no getting out of the betrothal, my lord. No matter if you wish it otherwise."

"We were children, Matilda." He shook his head as if seeking the words to make her understand. "It was a promise made in youthful folly, and I should have corrected her notion years ago, but I thought she would marry. I thought she forgot about our silly promises, but I see now that she did not." He clasped her hands, his grip firm. "I'm in love with you. I want to marry you and no one else."

Matilda's resolve faltered, her heart aching at the raw sincerity in his eyes. "I will not be your mistress, and if you're not free to marry, that is all that is open for me. I will not lose everything to be with you, as much as I may wish to. I could not do that to my family, friends, or myself."

"And I'm not asking you to be my mistress. I will not marry anyone unless it is you. I will fix my errors. I will make Lady Delphine see sense, and we will be together."

"And if she does not? If her family refuses to

see that your youthful love was nothing more than a passing phase?"

"I will make them see, or I shall simply steal you away, and we will marry in Gretna. We're both of age. No one can stop us or make us annul the marriage." His fingers squeezed hers, and she reveled in the feel of his warm hands. "I love you. I will not allow anyone to make me give you up."

The words hung in the air, their weight pressing against the walls of her heart. Matilda stared up at him, her breath shallow as his confession settled over her and began to seem genuine.

"You love me, truly?" She wanted to believe his words but was scared his confession and promises were as hollow as her future felt but hours ago.

"Yes, I do." He cupped her cheek. His touch was warm, his palm calloused yet gentle as his thumb brushed against her skin. "I love you, Lady Matilda Bligh. And I am done pretending that I do not."

Matilda surged toward him, her hands clutching at his coat as she pressed her lips to his. The kiss was a rush of fire and desperation, their pent-up emotions pouring forth in a wave neither could contain.

Christopher's arms wrapped around her, pulling her close as he deepened the kiss. The fire's heat paled compared to the blaze between them, their bodies moving as if drawn by an unseen force.

Christopher scooped Matilda into his arms, his strength effortlessly lifting her as he carried her toward the bed. The warmth of his body seeped through the layers of her gown, igniting a thrill of anticipation that made her heart race. He set her down, his lips finding hers, his kisses both demanding and tender, as his fingers moved to the row of buttons lining her bodice.

With practiced ease, he unfastened her gown, his touch reverent as he peeled away the yards of fabric that cascaded to the floor in a whisper of silk and lace. Matilda's breath hitched as she reached for his coat, pushing it from his shoulders and letting it fall with a muted thud. Her trembling fingers worked at the knot of his cravat, tossing it aside before tackling the buttons of his waistcoat. The storm of their desire left no room for hesitation, their hands moving with urgency as they stripped each other bare.

They tumbled onto the bed, and she wrapped her legs around his hips, wanting him with an urgency that would not wait.

He thrust into her, and she gasped, the stinging pain removing any desire she had for a breath or two. Christopher paused and watched her, a small frown between his brows.

"I'm sorry. I got carried away and forgot that you are a maid."

She nodded and, after several calming breaths, wiggled a little beneath him. He bit his lip, a muscle working in his jaw and she wished she knew what he was thinking. Was he enjoying her? Did her adjusting to his size hurt him, or did it bring him pleasure?

She knew that in time, she, too, would enjoy this interlude. Her friends had told her the joys of the marriage bed after the initial coupling, which could be trying.

She shifted again, seeking him, and he kissed her, removing the last of her apprehensions. He drove into her, and this time, there was no pain, just delicious heat, fulfillment, and a sweet ache that grew with each thrust.

"Christopher..." She was delirious for him. After tonight, there would be no going back. She would not lose him to another. Christopher would be her husband and she did not care what scandal that created.

She could not lose him again.

He was a magnificent lover and seemed to play her body like a virtuoso of lovemaking. The pinnacle of release teased and taunted her with each joining of their bodies. She ached to come with him deep within her, to satisfy the need that ran wild in her blood.

He pulled out, and before she could ask him what he was about, he was kneeling between her legs, pressing her knees apart and enjoying the view.

His eyes burned with desire and determination. She shivered as he pressed sweet kisses to her aching, wet flesh. His tongue worked her until she did not know how to survive the onslaught of his wickedness.

"Yes..." she breathed, fisting his hair in her hands, attempting to remain tethered to this beautiful earth by any means possible. "Christopher, I'm going to..."

Lights flashed before her eyes and she climaxed with him licking and loving her most private place. She undulated against his mouth, a wanton as she drew out every last delectable moment of her release.

He came back over her, her body heightened to his touch. He kneaded her breast as he licked along her bottom lip. "You are so mouthwatering. I will never not want you."

Her skin prickled and she kissed him, reveling in the taste of her pleasure on his lips. He thrust into her, pumping relentlessly before he found his own release. His body tightened, the muscles of his back like stone, his breath ragged as he spilled into her.

"Matilda," he gasped.

She cupped his face and watched as he came, wanting to see the ecstasy that they both shared wash over his face. He was so handsome and dear to her that she would forever want him, too.

After several minutes of catching their breath, Christopher broke apart and lay beside her, their foreheads resting together as they clung to each other.

"Say it again," Matilda whispered. "I want to hear those three fabulous words again."

"I love you," he said without hesitation. A shiver slipped down her spine hearing his declaration. "I love you and will do whatever it takes to make you mine, to make you happy."

Tears slid down her cheeks, but this time, they were tears of joy. "I love you too." His lopsided smile at her response made her love him even more. "I have for so long, Christopher. I was so afraid I'd lost you."

"Never!" He reached for her, cradling her face. "You'll never lose me, Matilda. I'll fight for you, for us. Whatever it takes."

He kissed her again, slower this time, the urgency giving way to something deeper. His hands roamed over her back, his touch igniting every nerve as he pulled her closer.

The fire crackled in the hearth, the storm outside forgotten as they lost themselves in each other.

"You are so beautiful," he murmured, brushing a strand of hair from her face.

Matilda reached up, her fingers tracing the strong line of his jaw. "And you are everything I never dared to hope for."

They kissed again, their movements slow and deliberate as they explored the depths of their connection. The world outside ceased to exist, leaving only the two of them in the quiet cocoon of their love.

As the night wore on, they spoke in whispers, their words filled with promises of a brighter future. They talked of life together, the joy they would find in each other's arms, and the strength they would draw from their love.

"I will never let you go," Christopher vowed. "Tomorrow, we shall return to the ducal estate, and I will right the wrong I caused all those years ago."

"And I will stand by you, no matter what." Matilda clasped his hand, needing to reassure him, and mayhap, herself a little too.

CHAPTER
TWENTY-SIX

Their return to the estate was not without its complications. They sat before his father's mahogany desk in his library. His parents, along with Lord and Lady Haverly and Lady Delphine, greeted them with a mixture of raised brows and disappointed glowers.

Lady Delphine's the severest of them all.

"This is most improper." Lady Delphine's sharp gaze cut to where Christopher's hand clasped Matilda's and narrowed farther. "Lady Matilda is entirely capable of continuing her journey without you running off behind her to drag her back here. You should not have bothered, Lord Charteris."

"She was stranded and is one of our family's closest friends, not to mention the Duke and Duchess Lane-Fox's only daughter. I could not leave her there to be at risk of every blaggard who required a roof in the storm." Christopher's response was curt and to the point, but he could not stomach the idea of Matilda in danger. "What would you have me do? Leave her at the mercy of fortune hunters?"

Delphine sniffed. "She is hardly helpless. You risk scandal by bringing her into this house. What if someone saw you, chaperoned only by her maid. You would be forced to marry her, and then you would not get to marry me, which is what you want, of course."

"Scandal be damned," Christopher snapped. "I would rather face a thousand wagging tongues than see harm come to Matilda."

Delphine said no more, retreating with a huff.

"Speaking of which, there will be no marriage between us, Lady Delphine. I never proposed, and there was never an engagement."

"I beg your pardon." Lord Haverly's tone was soft but with an edge of frost. "I do believe you're mistaken, Lord Charteris."

Matilda, who had remained silent throughout the exchange, cast Christopher a concerned glance. He squeezed her fingers, silently vowing that he would do whatever it took to protect her—even if it meant defying his family and society itself.

"I do not agree, and I am correct in my statement," Christopher said, holding Matilda's hand firmly. "You cannot expect me to marry a woman I offered for when we were both children. What Lady Delphine fails to understand is that the youthful friendship we had was never love. I know this now because my love for the woman beside me is far greater than anything I ever thought possible. I will not lose her, and I will not be forced into marriage to appease anyone—not even family or friends."

"You offered, Lord Charteris," Lord Haverly blustered, his face reddening with indignation. "Marriages have been arranged between people far younger than when you were both young adults. Your argument holds no merit."

"We do not live in the sixteenth century, Lord Haverly," Christopher countered. "This is the eighteenth century, and modern, sensible thinking must prevail. While I regret disappointing Lady Delphine, I will not marry her. I do not love her as a husband should, and despite my efforts to make her understand during your stay here, she refused to listen."

Sitting across the room, his mother glanced at Lady Delphine, concern evident in her furrowed brow. Christopher hoped that his parents might be swayed to his cause.

"The announcement at the picnic was made without my approval or knowledge," Christopher continued. "It has already hurt the woman I do wish to marry—a woman I love beyond words and will not lose."

"This is disgraceful behavior!" Lord Haverly thundered, rising to his feet. "You offered for my daughter, and she accepted your proposal. That should be the end of it. You will do the right thing by Delphine and everyone in this room—including Lady Matilda—whose father, I am certain, would not want his daughter embroiled in scandal."

Christopher's heart stuttered at the mention of Matilda's father. The thought of her suffering any repercussions because of his past foolishness filled him with dread.

"I will not be held accountable as an adult for a child's fanciful, impulsive promise." Christopher's voice held steady even though his chest burned with frustration. He turned to the duke. "Father, surely you cannot expect me to marry a woman I do not love. You know this is wrong."

His Grace's expression remained inscrutable. He exchanged a glance with his wife before speaking. "You claim to love Lady Matilda? You have not known her long. Are you certain of your feelings?"

Christopher's jaw tightened. "I am. I cannot breathe unless she is by my side. When she left, it felt as though a part of me had ceased to exist. You are right; we have not known each other long, but I know what I feel is true." He turned to Matilda, his heart filling at the sight of her. "I love and adore her."

Matilda's eyes shimmered with unshed tears, her lips parting to speak, but Lady Delphine's wailing pierced the air, shattering the tender moment.

"I waited years!" Delphine cried in a shrill voice. "I became an old maid waiting for you! And this is how you repay me? You're a cad, Lord Charteris, and I will ensure all of London knows it. I will ruin your perfect little Lady Matilda. No respectable home will admit her."

"You will do no such thing." Christopher fought not to sound cold and hostile, but he would not have Matilda threatened. "Lady Matilda is a duke's daughter and outranks you. To make her your enemy would be folly. I have been patient, Lady Delphine, but I will not tolerate baseless threats against the woman I love."

"Your Graces," Lady Haverly interjected, desperation in her words. She turned to the Duke and Duchess of D'Estel, "you cannot allow this engagement to end. Yes, they were young when they fell in love, but it was love. You must make your son honor his word."

The duchess remained composed, her gaze fixed on Christopher. "Are you certain of this, my son?" she asked in a measured tone he'd often heard from his mother when she was trying to reconcile a situation. "There will be talk. Homes that once welcomed you may close their doors. Are you prepared to face that?"

"I am," Christopher replied without hesitation. He raised his chin, his resolve unshakable. "I will not give up Lady Matilda. I tried to remain aloof, to hide behind the guise of a bachelor, but I can no longer deceive myself. I love her and will not conceal that love merely to ease the hurt this misunderstanding has caused." He turned to Delphine, remorseful to have caused her pain. "I tried to tell you, Delphine, but you would not listen. I never meant to hurt you, but my heart has never been yours. I am truly sorry."

Lady Delphine's lip trembled, but anger soon replaced sorrow. "Outrageous," Lord Haverly barked, striding toward the door. "Consider this friendship at an end! Your son has disgraced us and treated my daughter with contempt. I hope you are proud."

The Duke of D'Estel rose, his face stern. "We are disappointed by the situation," he said, "but we will not force a union that would bring unhappiness to both parties. It is time for Lady Delphine to seek her match, Lord Haverly. Your friendship with our family is not worth perpetuating this farce."

Lord Haverly's face darkened, but he said nothing as he wrenched the door open. Lady Haverly trailed after him, her expression stricken, while Lady Delphine shot one last venomous glare at Matilda before flouncing out of the room.

The silence that followed was heavy, the tension lingering like a storm that had just passed. Christopher turned to his parents, his shoulders straight. "I am sorry for the trouble this has caused."

Matilda stepped forward, her hands clasped before her. "We never intended to hurt anyone," she said, her voice strained, much like the day had been. "But we cannot deny our feelings. I love your son, and I want to be his wife."

His mother's expression softened, and she approached Matilda, pulling her into a warm embrace. "Now, now, my dear, we are not angry with you." The duchess's tone was kind and in much need of hearing right at this moment. "In fact, we are quite pleased with Christopher's choice."

Matilda blinked, stunned. "Truly?"

The duchess smiled, her eyes twinkling with warmth. "While I was pleased at the thought of an engagement to Lady Delphine, it was only because I wished for my son to find happiness—and to give me grandchildren before I am too old to enjoy them!" She laughed softly, then glanced at Christopher. "But now, seeing the two of you together, I have no doubt that you belong with each other."

The Duke of D'Estel nodded, stepping forward to clasp Christopher's shoulder. "Your happiness is what matters most. We are proud of you for standing firm."

Relief washed over Christopher, and he took Matilda's hand, pulling her close. "Thank you." He cleared his throat from the tightness he felt here. "I believe we shall be very happy indeed."

Matilda looked up at him, her smile radiant. "The merriest."

And for the first time in days, Christopher felt the weight on his heart begin to lift.

CHAPTER
TWENTY-SEVEN

They were married in the grand drawing room of the ducal estate, the elegant space adorned with garlands of summer roses and sprays of jasmine that filled the air with their sweet fragrance. Sunlight poured in through tall windows, catching the gilded edges of the room's ornate moldings and casting a warm glow over the gathered guests.

The wedding breakfast in the adjoining ballroom reminded Matilda of Charlotte's celebration just a few weeks prior, though this day felt infinitely more magical. Long tables were set with gleaming silverware and delicate china, each place marked by a sprig of lavender tied with a ribbon in the couple's ivory and pale-blue colors. Despite the unseasonably warm summer weather, the atmosphere indoors was light and cheerful, with laughter and the clinking of glasses filling the room.

"Happy?" Christopher whispered, leaning

down to kiss her, uncaring of the many eyes on them. His hand rested possessively at her waist as though to remind her—and himself—that they now belonged to each other.

Matilda tilted her face to his, her cheeks burning at his show of public affection. "So very happy," she murmured, unable to stop the smile that had tilted her lips for days. "I didn't know it was possible to feel this much."

He chuckled and sipped her champagne. "Mayhap, we could sneak away after dinner and relive our first intimate encounter at the river. I could use a cold dip in the water after the warm day."

Matilda grinned, loving how well that sounded. "I would love to go for a swim, but will not your family notice we're missing?"

"Trust me." Christopher kissed the top of her head. "They will not be looking for us on our wedding night."

Her stomach fluttered at the thought of what was to come before she took a sip of her champagne. She did not wish to count down the hours of their wedding breakfast but was also keen to be alone with her new husband.

Before she could reply, a stir rippled through the room. The murmur of conversation faltered as the crowd parted, revealing Lady Delphine standing in the doorway. Her cheeks were flushed, not with happiness but with a simmering fury that seemed to vibrate in the tension of her stance.

"Lady Delphine." Christopher instinctively stepped in front of Matilda, wanting to protect her from any insults.

"Do not *Lady Delphine* me," she snapped, her tone high-pitched and brittle. "I came to wish the bride my sincerest congratulations."

The sarcasm in her words were like a blade, sharp enough to draw a collective gasp from the guests. Delphine stalked forward, her elaborate gown rustling like an approaching tempest. On a nearby table sat the wedding cake, a towering masterpiece of sugared flowers and delicate piping. Delphine's gaze locked on to it, and before anyone could react, she seized a slice from the display.

"You may have his ring," Delphine spat, glaring at Matilda. "But you'll never have his honor." With a wild motion, she hurled the cake at Matilda.

The crowd erupted in gasps, a shocked silence falling as the frosted slice struck Matilda's bodice.

"That is enough!" His voice was a thunderclap in the stunned room. He signaled to the footmen, who quickly flanked Lady Delphine. "You will leave at once."

Delphine's expression twisted with a mix of rage and despair, but when she realized no one in the room was coming to her defense, she straightened. "You'll regret this, Lord Charteris," she hissed as the footmen escorted her out. "You have not heard the last from me."

A ripple of uneasy murmurs filled the room as the doors closed behind his once-childhood friend. Christopher turned back to Matilda, his gaze filled with worry. "Are you all right?"

Matilda brushed at the smear of frosting on her gown, smiling through the dramatic interruption. "It seems Lady Delphine wasn't fond of the cake," she quipped, earning a laugh from a few nearby guests.

Christopher cupped her face, his thumb brushing her cheek. "I'm so sorry. She had no right—"

"She's gone," Matilda interrupted. "And I have everything I could ever want and nothing to be ashamed of. While I feel for Lady Delphine, I do not think she is thinking clearly right now, but I hope we can be friends one day."

"As do I," Christopher agreed.

The breakfast resumed with a renewed air of celebration, and when no one was watching, Christopher leaned down and whispered into Matilda's ear, "Come with me."

Moments later, they escaped the ballroom, their laughter echoing about the grounds as they slipped into the sprawling gardens. The heat of the day had given way to a balmy, golden afternoon. Christopher led Matilda to the lake at the edge of the estate, its surface shimmering under the late sunlight.

"Shall we go for a swim?" he asked, smiling at the memory of their first time here?"

Matilda grinned, kicking off her shoes and placing her bare toes into the soft grass as she approached the river. "How could I forget? You were so determined to stop me from swimming. Trying to scare me off with your talk of drowning."

Christopher laughed, the gratifying sound rich and carefree. "And you, my lady, were far too independent and stubborn to heed my warning."

She tilted her head, grinning. "Shall we relive the memory?"

Before Christopher could answer, Matilda reached for the hooks and eyes at the front of her gown, her fingers moving with a mix of excitement and anticipation. The fabric pooled at her feet in a cascade of cream silk. Her petticoat and false rump were easy to remove, but she paused, turning her back to Christopher for assistance with her stays.

He stepped closer, his warm hands brushing against her as he worked the cord, untying it with haste. With each loosened knot, her breaths deepened, free of the constraint. The stays slipped from her shoulders, leaving only the soft linen of her underpetticoat and shift. One by one, those too were shed, along with her stockings, until she stood bare beneath the twilight sky.

The warm sunset air embraced her like a silken shawl. Matilda glanced at Christopher as he removed his clothes, his movements confident and unhurried. The light played over his strong, chiseled form, highlighting every line of the man who was now hers in every sense.

Her husband.

The thought filled her with a profound joy that nearly brought tears to her eyes. How odd and wonderful it sounded, yet how effortlessly right it felt.

Christopher reached for her hand, his touch grounding her in the moment. Together, they ran down the dock, their laughter carrying over the still water before they leaped into the lake. The water's cool embrace shocked their skin, drawing a gasp from Matilda.

They surfaced together, their faces mere inches apart. She gazed at him, her heart swelling with love and desire. They swam lazily for a time, their playful splashes punctuated by laughter. But soon, Christopher reached for her, pulling her into his arms. His hands found her waist, as his lips claimed hers in a slow, deep, and all-consuming kiss.

"I love you," he murmured. "I will spend every day of my life making sure you never doubt that."

Tears prickled Matilda's eyes as she cupped his face, her fingertips tracing the angles she had come to cherish. "And I love you. You've given me a happiness I never dreamed possible when I first came to stay with your sister. You were the most wonderful and unexpected surprise."

Her fingers trailed over his chest, his strong

beating heart a steady rhythm beneath her palm. With a sudden motion, he lifted her, and she wrapped her legs instinctively around his waist.

As she sank onto him, her breath hitched, the fullness of him igniting a sweet ache that coursed through her body. Christopher sucked in a breath, his gaze dark with reverence and longing.

"You're so beautiful," his said unsteadily. "I'm so thankful you're mine."

His words made her heart sing. "And I love how you make me feel," she teased, a playful smile curving her lips. "Has anyone ever mentioned how skilled you are at this?"

His wide eyes and the chuckle that followed told her she had taken him by surprise. "No," he admitted, his grin returning. "And nor have I ever asked."

She grinned

"You're wicked," he growled, "and I adore that about you."

She began to move, her body finding a rhythm that matched his. Each movement sent ripples through the lake, their union mirrored in the shimmering reflection on the water's surface.

"You're not looking to change me, then?" she asked, hoping that was the case and that she had chosen right. That the man she had placed all her trust and love in would not disappoint her.

"Hell no, I'm not. I want you to remain just as you are—full of fire and life, independent and opinionated. I couldn't stomach anything less. You are a marvel, Matilda, and I'm in awe of you."

"You're a flatterer," she murmured, her hands tangling in his damp hair. "But don't you change, either. I love you just as you are, too."

He tightened his hold on her, his thrusts growing deeper and more deliberate. "And I love how you feel in my arms," he groaned, his lips brushing against hers. "When I'm deep within you, nothing else matters."

The heat between them built to a crescendo, their teasing words giving way to moans and sighs of pleasure. The tension inside her coiled tighter with every thrust, her body trembling as she neared the precipice.

"Come for me," he commanded. His eyes locked on to hers, a rule to do as he said. "Let go, my love."

The words, spoken with such authority and devotion, sent her spiraling into release. Her body arched against his, her cry echoing across the still lake as waves of pleasure overtook her. Christopher followed moments later, groaning her name as he buried his face against her neck. His shuddering breaths warmed her skin. The sound of his satisfaction sent another shiver down her spine.

They remained entwined, their bodies weightless in the water as they clung to each other, letting the remnants of their passion ebb and flow around them.

"I will never tire of this," Matilda whispered, her fingers tracing lazy patterns on his damp shoulder.

He kissed her, a smile tugging at his lips. "Nor will I. This is only the beginning, my love."

Matilda felt a contentment she had never known as they remained entwined in the water. The life ahead of them stretched out like the calm expanse of the lake, filled with possibilities, love, and the unshakable promise that they would always face its challenges together.

EPILOGUE

Matilda cradled Genevieve's little son, holding him snugly against her shoulder as she gently patted his tiny back. The soft cotton of his baby gown tickled her arm, and his sweet, milky scent filled the room, warming her heart. After a blissful month of marriage, she and Christopher had traveled to Genevieve and Lord Tyndall's estate, joining Charlotte and Lord Lacy for a delightful visit.

The past week had been a perfect blend of simple joys—hours spent doting on Genevieve's newborn, Lord Alaric, followed by evenings of wine, laughter, and lively conversations with her dearest friends. The estate, bathed in the golden hues of early February light, felt like a haven.

"I still cannot believe you're a mama." Charlotte leaned over Matilda to stroke Lord Alaric's velvety cheek. Her fingers lingered, marveling at the baby's softness.

Genevieve smiled radiantly, her eyes never

straying far from her infant son. "Neither can I," she admitted, her voice brimming with awe and affection. "I never imagined how full my heart could feel. He's such a content little thing. I already dream of giving him a brother or sister—imagine how wonderful it would be to have a house full of little ones!"

"The sweetest thought," Charlotte agreed, sipping her tea, steam curling above the delicate china cup. She gestured to the terrace, where their husbands stood, talking animatedly on the frost-covered flagstones, the morning sun catching on the dew-kissed garden behind them. "What do you suppose they're discussing out there?"

Matilda shifted Lord Alaric in her arms, his rosebud lips slightly parted in sleep. The weight of him, warm and trusting in her embrace, brought a surge of tenderness. "Likely horses or estate matters. Or perhaps debating which of them is more pleased with their lot in life." She smiled, tilting her head to gaze fondly at Christopher. "Can you believe that this time last year, none of us were married?"

Charlotte let out a soft laugh. "Unmarried, without even a suitor to our names. And now look at us—one of us a mama, and the other two happily wed. It feels almost too good to be true."

"A lovely dream indeed," Genevieve chimed in, her gaze turning to her husband. Her eyes softened with the unmistakable glow of love.

Matilda watched her friends. Their happiness

so palpable it seemed to infuse the air. A warmth swelled in her chest as she glanced between Genevieve, Charlotte, and the men who had claimed their hearts.

"I know Christopher is your brother, Charlotte," Matilda said, "but I do not know what I would have done had I not married him. Just the thought of him being with another..." She shivered involuntarily. "It would be unbearable. He's my other half. I can't imagine life without him now."

Charlotte reached out, squeezing Matilda's hand. "I know. And the good news is that Lady Delphine will not be causing a scene during this year's London Season. Mama sent word—she's engaged! It seems her cousin began courting her, and the two fell in love. A much happier end to what was a prickly situation."

"How lovely," Genevieve said, sighing in relief.

"Indeed," Matilda agreed. She smiled as her gaze shifted back to the terrace, where Christopher caught her eye and winked. Her heart fluttered.

The men rejoined them moments later, their heavy boots clunking softly on the polished wood floor. Lord Lacy leaned forward to pour himself a cup of tea while Christopher moved to Matilda's side, settling into the chair beside her.

"He is adorable, is he not?" Christopher murmured in her ear, his breath warm against her skin as he gazed at the sleeping baby in her arms.

Matilda turned toward Christopher. "He is indeed. And I would love to give you a son," she teased. "Soon perhaps..."

Christopher's hand found hers, his thumb brushing lightly over her knuckles. He raised her hand to his lips, kissing it softly. "And I would love for you to be a mama. Mayhap this afternoon, we might start working toward that goal." His lips quirked into a mischievous grin. "It has been far too many hours since I've held you in my arms, my love."

Matilda's cheeks warmed at his audacity. "Miss me already, Christopher?"

"Always," he replied without hesitation.

She shivered at the promise she heard in his tone. The idea of retreating to their room and indulging in his touch was tempting, far too tempting to resist. She arched a brow, her smile playful. "Very well, my darling. Let us retire this afternoon—there's no need to sneak about."

His dark eyes burned with promise as they locked on hers, a slow smile spreading across his face. "I will count the minutes, my love."

"As will I," she replied, her heart thrumming with anticipation.

The couple excused themselves not long after luncheon, and the warmth of their shared anticipation carried them up the grand staircase to their room. Once inside, Christopher wasted no time, scooping Matilda into his arms. She laughed in delight.

"Shall we pick up where we left off, Lady

Charteris?" he teased, kissing the tip of her nose in affection.

"Only if you promise not to let me go," she countered, her arms winding around his neck.

"Never," he vowed, his lips finding hers in a deep, lingering kiss. "For this lifetime and the next."

DON'T MISS TAMARA'S OTHER ROMANCE SERIES

Heiress

Diamond of the Season

Treasure of the Ton

Jewel of the Ball

1777 Society

One Night in London

Midnight in Mayfair

An Evening to Remember

Dalliance and Dukes

My Virtuous Duke

My Notorious Rogue

My Ruthless Beau

The Wayward Yorks

A Wager with a Duke

My Reformed Rogue

Wild, Wild, Duke

In the Duke of Time

Duke Around and Find Out

The Wayward Woodvilles

A Duke of a Time

On a Wild Duke Chase

Speak of the Duke

Every Duke has a Silver Lining

One Day my Duke Will Come

Surrender to the Duke

My Reckless Earl

Brazen Rogue

The Notorious Lord Sin

Wicked in My Bed

League of Unweddable Gentlemen

Tempt Me, Your Grace

Hellion at Heart

Dare to be Scandalous

To Be Wicked With You

Kiss Me, Duke

The Marquess is Mine

Kiss the Wallflower

A Midsummer Kiss

A Kiss at Mistletoe

A Kiss in Spring

To Fall For a Kiss

A Duke's Wild Kiss

To Kiss a Highland Rose

To Marry a Rogue

Only an Earl Will Do

Only a Duke Will Do

Only a Viscount Will Do

Only a Marquess Will Do

Only a Lady Will Do

Lords of London

To Bedevil a Duke

To Madden a Marquess

To Tempt an Earl

To Vex a Viscount

To Dare a Duchess

To Marry a Marchioness

Royal House of Atharia

To Dream of You

A Royal Proposition

Forever My Princess

A Time Traveler's Highland Love

To Conquer a Scot

To Save a Savage Scot

To Win a Highland Scot

A Stolen Season

A Stolen Season

A Stolen Season: Bath

A Stolen Season: London

Scandalous London

A Gentleman's Promise

A Captain's Order

A Marriage Made in Mayfair

High Seas & High Stakes

His Lady Smuggler

Her Gentleman Pirate

A Wallflower's Christmas Wreath

Daughters Of The Gods

Banished

Guardian

Fallen

Stand Alone Books

Defiant Surrender

A Brazen Agreement

To Sin with Scandal

Outlaws

ABOUT THE AUTHOR

Tamara is an Australian author who grew up in an old mining town in country South Australia, where her love of history was founded. So much so, she made her darling husband travel to the UK for their honeymoon, where she dragged him from one historical monument and castle to another.

A mother of three, her two little gentlemen in the making, a future lady (she hopes) keep her busy in the real world, but whenever she gets a moment's peace she loves to write romance novels in an array of genres, including regency, medieval and time travel.

Made in the USA
Columbia, SC
21 February 2025